YOUNG FU
of the upper yangtze

YOUNG FU
of the upper yangtze

by Elizabeth Foreman Lewis
illustrated by Ed Young

introduction by Pearl S. Buck

A Yearling Book

Published by
Bantam Doubleday Dell Books for Young Readers
a division of
Bantam Doubleday Dell Publishing Group, Inc.
1540 Broadway
New York, New York 10036

YOUNG FU OF THE UPPER YANGTZE has been translated into
the following foreign languages: Czech, Danish, Norwegian, Dutch,
Finnish, German, Afrikaans, Polish, Spanish, and Swedish, as well
as having been published in Great Britain.

ISBN: 0-440-49043-X

Reprinted by arrangement with Henry Holt and Company, Inc.

Printed in the United States of America

One Previous Edition

February 1990

10   9

OPM

to MY HUSBAND
and MY SON

CONTENTS

INTRODUCTION

To understand and enjoy a book about a country and its people, it is always necessary to know something, however general, of their history and their ways of living and thinking, which is to say their culture. At the present moment in our world this necessity is especially true in regard to China, one of the oldest countries.

Chin Shih Huang was China's first emperor, thousands of years ago—to be exact, his dynasty was from 220 B.C. to A.D. 207. At that time China was not one country but six countries, all trying to live together in peace, but more often actually at war. The ambitious young king of the country called Chin decided to make war on all the other countries and establish them under his rule as First Emperor. He attacked country by country, until at last he ruled them all and governed an entire vast nation.

Chin Shih Huang established China as we know it today, and the pattern is clear through the centuries. Dynasty followed dynasty in the same imperial fashion, only twice broken by foreign conquerors but always regained by the Chinese. Of course there were periods of chaos as one dynasty merged into another, and it was in such a period of change that I lived most of my long life in China, beginning when I was three months old, when my parents took me to China with them, and where I lived until I was more than forty years old. It is in this period that Elizabeth Lewis has placed her story of YOUNG FU.

What kind of a period was it? It was a period of revolution, struggle, and wars. The old empress, Tzu Hsi, died in 1909. Immediately contenders for the Imperial Throne rose up, each with his private army, to fight all others, one by one. These contenders, bold ambitious men, were called *tuchun*. Each ruled temporarily in his area until another drove him away. Meanwhile, the people waited until one final conqueror would prove himself victor over all the others and become the first emperor of a new dynasty. Such periods were always dangerous, for robbers roamed and rascals thrived. This book tells of such troubles. People's lives and businesses were always unsafe, and there was often little difference, if any, between a bandit and a soldier. People were killed in their homes and shops, and only the very poor were safe.

Young Fu's life, so well portrayed by Elizabeth Lewis, was in the years of turmoil, after the old empress died. In this disorganized period he did his best to live an honest, hardworking life, and it is his story that is here told with faithful attention to the difficult and dangerous times in which he lived. To understand the vast, complex China of today, one must try to learn about its past. The story of Young Fu of the Upper Yangtze is a prologue to modern China.

Pearl S. Buck

Danby, Vermont
October, 1972

YOUNG FU
of the upper yangtze

A CITY
SET
UPON
A HILL

YOUNG FU stood on the narrow curbing before Dai's two-storied tenement in Chair-Makers' Way, Chung-king, and stared about him. In the doorway, Fu Be Be, his mother, directed load-coolies in placing the household goods which she had brought from home, and anxiously examined each article as it passed before her.

A day of clattering over country roads, followed by two on the crowded freight boat, had been difficult indeed for her, but the furniture looked no worse for wear than did her son. For him the hours had flowed into the past as swiftly as the current of the river. He had been fascinated by shifting scenes and strange faces; the constant menace of bandits with which all travel was shadowed, had added its own flavor to the experience, and when at last Chungking's great walls had loomed above them, it had seemed the fulfillment of all his dreams.

He turned in the direction of a yell as one of the load-bearers lowered his burden of a pigskin trunk on the bare foot of a bystander. In a flash the two men, their faces white with anger, were after each other.

"Pig, have you no eyes?"

"And you, grandson of a two-headed dog, could you not see that trunk?"

"It is your affair, you whose ancestors for ten generations have been scavengers of the streets, to look where you place a load!"

"And it is yours, whose grandmother resembled a monkey, to move out of the way of workers!"

The carrier, unlike the Chungkingese about him, wore a queue, and the bystander stretched out a hand, grabbed the tail of hair, and pulled viciously. The queue, half of which was false hair plaited in with string, came apart in his hand and the onlookers roared. Furious with chagrin, the victim lifted his carrying pole to strike. As he did so, an unexpected clamor in the street drew everyone's attention, and the bystander seized this opportunity to lose himself in the crowd.

A handsome red wedding chair, ornately decorated with gold, rolled past. Hidden completely behind its satin-hung curtains, sat a youthful bride on the way to her new home. A long train of coolies followed the chair, swinging great, painted trays on which rested roast fowls and sweetmeats, silk bed comforts and hard, lacquered pillows, sealed boxes of clothing, and pieces of furniture—all of the contributions essential to any dowry. When the last of these had disappeared from sight, the angry carrier, who had succeeded in plaiting his queue to its original length, stooped, picked up his pole, and resumed work as if nothing had ever disturbed him.

Fu Be Be breathed a sigh of relief. After the quiet countryside, this city was providing more excitement than she could well endure, but she would have to be content for her son's sake.

Young Fu, unconscious of anything but the fact that he was now in Chungking, drew a long breath of delight. In his village men who counted it a privilege to visit this city once in a lifetime had told of its wonders.

"Miles of streets there are, lined with shops where may be purchased more than any man will ever need," he had heard the innkeeper say one evening. "The people, a hundred times ten thousand in number—so many that they are forced to build dwellings on top of one another that all may be sheltered—work at their

A handsome red wedding chair rolled past.

countless trades and, when there is time for play, enjoy themselves in handsome tea houses and theaters." Here the speaker had paused in the act of serving a new customer and had gazed inquiringly from one listener to another. "When, sirs," he had demanded, "do farmers and innkeepers ever find time to play? Certainly the citizens of that place are people of good fortune!"

A true saying! For Chungking, built high above the waters that swept about its feet, was distinct in its position of port city to all of this far, western world. To the west and north towered the frozen Himalayas and mysterious Tibet; to the south, trade routes, centuries old, connected it with Indo-China, Burma, and India; to the east, its main artery of life, the Yangtze-kiang, flowed tortuously for fifteen hundred miles before it reached Shanghai and the coast and emptied its muddy stream into the blue Pacific.

And, ancient and gray, Chungking opened its gates to let the tides of commerce flow in and out, never failing to reach for the choicest prizes and hug them to itself. Wealth it had, wealth that was reckoned enormous even in Szechuen, this the richest province in the Middle Kingdom, and poverty such as only an overpopulated Chinese city can know. Young Fu's pulse quickened; he, Fu Yuin-fah, at the age of thirteen was already here, standing on one of its streets and watching coolies carry familiar household possessions into the room in which he and his mother would live.

That Fu Be Be did not share his enthusiasm, he knew.

For weeks she had wept over the idea of leaving the farm land where she had spent her life. But with her husband's death, she had not known in which direction to turn for help. Her father-in-law had died years before, and there was no other member of his family on whom she had a claim. Tilling the ground offered in these troubled times a secure living to no man. As for a widow and a growing boy—she clicked her tongue in dismay.

And then, when the future had seemed darkest, the Head of the Village told her of an opening for an apprentice with one Tang, a coppersmith of Chungking, and, at her request, letters had been exchanged and her son accepted. A life in Chungking was not what she would have chosen for either of them, but, as it was, she had not dared to refuse. Besides the meager furnishings of the farmhouse, she possessed only a few dollars and her wedding ornaments, silver hairpins and bracelets—a feeble barrier between themselves and hunger.

And now the square, red table, the rectangular stools, the rolled bedding, and the baskets of kitchen utensils had been carried within. Fu Be Be paid the coolies what they had been promised in advance and listened with small attention to their grumbling.

"This is not enough! These loads were twice as heavy as we thought them when we bargained price. You have robbed us of strength for the day. Give us another two hundred cash!"

"Two hundred cash!" she exclaimed. "Do I look like the widow of a mandarin? You agreed to my amount; if you are not satisfied, that is your affair." She waved them out of her way and entered the house.

The disgruntled coolies moved on down the street, and Young Fu turned with a sigh from the excitement of the curb. His momentary depression changed suddenly to a feeling of satisfaction that their room was in this lower house and not the upper. At the rear was a ladder which had to be climbed if one lived on top, and while that held no terrors for one who was used to scrambling to the roof of the farmhouse and adjusting tiles displaced by stormy winds, this business of living in the air above others was strange indeed. And for his mother, whose bound feet, four inches in length, had never been expected to step over anything higher than a door sill, this ladder would have presented a real problem.

Within, he stood and looked about. The walls of the one room which they were to occupy were plastered. In his village, the inn alone had plastered inner walls. That material cost more than plain baked clay, and if one could afford to have a wash of it on the outside of the building, it was a mark of prosperity. His own home had boasted such a coating and a tiled roof as well, but it had been built in his grandfather's day, when, for a brief period, the province had known peace and farmers had faced only the uncertainties of weather as their common enemy. His father had worked none the less diligently than his ancestors, but how could a man be expected to prosper when marching troops crushed the tender young plants in the fields, or settled in a village overnight and in that time seized a year's harvest for their use? Fowls and live stock disappeared always with the first visit of soldiers, and if they stayed away, the bandits came in their place.

"*Mi teh fah!*" his father had said in that expressive earth language which distinguished the talk of the farmers from that of their neighbors in the towns. "*Mi teh fah!*" And the men of the village had conquered their discouragement and planted again and again. But Young Fu, working from his sixth year beside his father in the fields, had watched him change from a young, good-humored man who was never too tired to laugh at the antics of his small assistant, to a bent, aging stranger with an unsmiling expression and lips that opened only to scold or cough. Here in Chungking there would be no farming worries at least.

Fu Be Be's voice prodded him into action. "Can you find nothing to do but stare? Certain it is there is little about this place worth anyone's glances."

Her son began to loosen ropes from a basket. "The walls are plastered," he suggested by way of favorable criticism.

His mother twisted her mouth. "Naturally, when houses are planted one on the other, something more than good, clean clay is needed. Wood or bamboo is doubtless beneath, but that will make it no better a place in which to live. Cracks there are in plenty, so that our neighbors' curiosity as well as their noise may enter. And holes! We shall do well if we do not supply food to any army of rats. Moreover, the light is poor. And I like not the odor." She walked to the rear and, pressing her

eye to a break in the wall, continued, "It is as I feared—
our landlord houses his pigs at the back."

In a short time the room was in order. Food was prepared and a candle lighted. It flickered grotesque shadows over the cracked walls, cast a soft glow on the
brass hot-water kettle which was Fu Be Be's special
pride, and reddened the highly colored countenance of
the genial kitchen god whose portrait had been placed
in a choice location on the chimney. This deity, friendly
though he was in appearance, had been known to carry
bad reports to Heaven at the festivities of the New Year
period, and it was wise for a household to give him the
place of honor on its walls.

Young Fu nodded wearily over the food. He held the
rice bowl close to his lips and with the chopsticks pushed
its contents into his packed jaws. Steaming tea revived
his interest in life. He became conscious of the ceaseless bustle of the street and, rising, slipped to the outer
door.

Chair-Makers' Way was busy about the preparation of
the evening meal and the approach of night. Load-
bearers carrying poles from which empty ropes now dan-
gled, beggars imploring pity, housewives attending to
last-minute errands, playing children, barking dogs—all
crowded the narrow street. The sedan-chair shops, that
gave to the place its name, were closing their fronts,
fitting into grooves the sliding wooden panels that
closed them in securely from the outer world. Patrons
thronged the hot-water stores, purchasing just enough
for a brewing of tea. To heat this for oneself was much

more expensive; that required a double purchase of cold water and charcoal.

With delight, Young Fu watched this activity. This was the life of which the visitors to Chungking had told. And tomorrow he would become an apprentice to Tang, the coppersmith, and when he had time for play, he would enjoy himself in tea houses and theaters. In a city like this, money for such pleasures would be easy to earn. He thought with a smile of pity of the existence to which his former companions in the village were condemned. Most of them would now be asleep, and their parents with them, while these people were still preparing evening rice. And instead of this interesting spectacle, there would be silence broken only by the frogs and an occasional howling dog.

"Good!" he said under his breath, "and great in fortune am I to be here."

"Truly?" a voice interrupted, and, startled, the boy looked up to find a tall, elderly figure beside him. A scholar—there was no doubt of that. Shabby of garment he was, but with the fine, intelligent expression with which even the youngest Chinese learns to associate a man versed in the Classic Wisdom. For further proof his hands, held carefully within each other, boasted nails three inches long on each of the smallest fingers, a sign that their owner engaged in no manual labor. He was smiling whimsically as he repeated, "Truly, thou dost think thy fortune great because thou hast come to live in this place?"

Young Fu, his cheeks red with the embarrassment of being overheard, bowed customarily three times, and stammered a reply, "Respected and Honored Sir, I am a newcomer in this city and its wonders seem very great to my stupid eyes."

The scholar nodded understandingly. "Thou art young and easy to please. Therein lies thy good fortune —in youth, not in coming to this city. Thou art from the country, is it not true?"

Young Fu bowed again. "You know all things, Revered One." Some of his first discomfort was wearing off. Never in his life had he held a personal conversation with a teacher; that this was happening now was only another example of the benefits to be derived from living in Chungking. He listened attentively to the other's continued speech.

"A good life it is to work with the soil and know the sun. That wilt thou not find in this city! It shines seldom and old bones like mine cry out for it. But thou wilt not miss it, not at first. Thou art strong." His eyes lightened with humor—"And good! That I can see for myself."

Young Fu, lost in interest, agreed soberly, then becoming aware of the old gentleman's amusement, his usual impudence rose above all other emotions. With a grin he replied, "Again you speak truly, Ancient One."

"A verity!" replied his elder, carrying on the spirit of the occasion, "and never hast thou been known to prod without warning thy neighbor's water buffalo, or to push a young companion on the slippery path between paddy

fields, or to torment thy mother for sugar cane and watermelon seeds, or to mock at thy elders when they were
not present."

Young Fu's attempt to affirm the reasonable quality
of these statements ended in laughter. His tormentor
smiled, then asked seriously, "What is thy name?"

"I am of the miserable house of Fu, and I answer to
Yuin-fah."

"And thou wilt dwell in this house, thou and thy
family?"

"I and my mother." The boy's expression became
shadowed by memory. "My father is no longer here."

There was a flash of sympathy, but no words concerning this loss.

"And thou wilt now care for thy mother?"

Young Fu answered proudly. "Tomorrow I go to be
an apprentice to one Tang, a coppersmith. I shall work
hard and my mother shall not want. Tang is, I understand, a man of importance in this city. It may be his
reputation is not unknown to you, sir."

"His name is not new to me. As an artisan, his stamp
on a piece of brass increases the price. Thou art fortunate to learn thy trade under his teaching." He turned
slightly. "My name is Wang, with the title, Scholar, of
which I am most unworthy. I dwell on the upper floor
of this house. If at any time thou shouldst meet with ill
fortune, as is sometimes true of a youth from the country, thou canst find me there in my room." In another
moment the dignified figure had moved to the rear of

the building and climbed the creaking treads to his apartment above.

The street was quieting. Most of the people had gone within their homes, and the shop fronts presented closed, wooden surfaces. An unexpected noise cut the silence. Four liveried coolies turned the corner and swung down the narrow way, a handsome sedan chair raised high on their shoulders. "Open the street!" they cried, "open the street for the rich foreigner!" From the curb a few feet away, a woman's shrill voice yelled, "Foreign devil! Foreign devil!" and the child, clinging to her hand, buried its face in its mother's clothing and whispered, "Foreign devil! Foreign devil! Foreign devil!"

Young Fu tingled. A foreigner had been in that chair. Never had he seen one of these strange creatures. They were said to come from lands so far away that their boundaries lay beyond the farthest reaches of the Middle Kingdom. All of this was puzzling indeed. In his village it was commonly believed that where the Middle Kingdom ended, there the world ended as well. And these foreigners were like the Miao and the Lo Lo, only another tribe of aboriginal savages. He had heard it said, also, that a great sea separated their land from China, though what a sea was, Young Fu was not at all sure. Water, perhaps like the Lin River; certainly nothing so large as the Yangtze-kiang, which was the greatest of its kind under Heaven. And here in this city foreigners were, no doubt, a common sight. He would make it his business soon to view one for himself. His mind felt about to burst with new experiences. The villagers had not told half of what was to be seen in Chungking.

He went within at a call from Fu Be Be, and closed the door carefully behind him. "A great scholar talked with me outside. He lives in this building. And I watched, only a minute ago, while a foreigner in a sedan chair rode past. It was too dark to see him," he finished with regret.

Fu Be Be drew her bed curtains and yawned wearily. "A scholar is a treasure under any rooftree, though why one should trouble to talk with you I do not know. May you copy his ways! As for foreigners, it is said that only evil comes to those who have dealings with them. Remember this when your curiosity would ruin you. Let us sleep! Tomorrow we rise early and call on your new master."

"IN THE BEGINNING ALL THINGS ARE DIFFICULT"

THE ROOM was quite dark when Fu Be Be's repeated callings aroused him. "What is it?" he asked sleepily.

"Already the Hour of the Tiger draws to a close. That we have moved to this city is no reason for your sleeping like a gentleman."

Young Fu sat up. "But it is still black as midnight."

He pulled the *pu-gai* about his shoulders. "Ai! it is cold."

"Laziness never filled a rice bowl. And Chungking is famous throughout the land for its bad weather, so I have heard." She shivered. "Cold it is." Loosening the latch, she glanced outside. "And the rain falls."

Yawning, her son struggled into his outer jacket. Fu Be Be was working over the dilapidated clay stove built into the chimney place. She rubbed stinging eyes as she blew the charcoal into flame. There was a breakfast of hard puffed rice. This, with hot water to drink, completed the meal. Then, dressed in their best garments, the boy and his mother set out for the coppersmith's.

Mist and fine rain lifted in the streets. Sedan chairs still bore lighted lanterns. A man carried a small oil lamp burning brightly. Its glass shade was wet. Young Fu looked after him. An uncovered light continuing to flame steadily in spite of falling water! This Chungking was different from that of the open country.

At Tang's, business was already in progress. They stood in admiration before the establishment. Trays and kettles, jars and vases, braziers and water pipes—everything that might be desired in white and yellow brass, or red-gold copper—were displayed on the shelves of the shop. An apprentice dusted stock and a clerk stood behind the counter and deftly counted with the wooden beads strung on the wires of an abacus. Before acknowledging the presence of these new arrivals, he laid down the frame, took up a small camel's-hair brush, dampened it leisurely on a black slab of ink, and wrote several characters in an account book.

At last he turned to Fu Be Be. "What do you wish?"

"To give this to your proprietor." She held out a long, narrow envelope.

He accepted it and addressed his assistant, "Take this, Den, to the master."

The boy laid aside the feather duster and moved to an inner room. As he did so, he eyed the two callers with a glance of derision. Young Fu reddened. He felt suddenly at a loss what to do with his hands and feet. With his chin he pointed to a table and two empty stools. "Let us sit," he suggested in a whisper.

Fu Be Be shook her head. "It is not custom; we have come to obtain work, not to buy."

After what seemed an hour, an older man appeared. He walked directly to them and spoke courteously. Behind him the apprentice, Den, stared in an unblinking gaze at the new applicant. Fu Be Be explained their errand.

"This is the youth of whom Wen, the farmer, wrote?"

Fu Be Be bowed.

"And his age?"

"Thirteen years and seven moons."

"That is older than I wish, but he has strength which apprentices sometimes lack." Without turning, he raised his voice, "This early in the day they are forced to rest a little."

The idler flushed guiltily and reached for the duster. Young Fu hid a smile. One thing was certain—this man missed nothing. His mother asked the coppersmith timidly about rules.

"The guild to which all of our artisans belong has in the past required five years of training for an apprentice, but at present, war changes conditions. The two I now have serve three years; your son may do the same. He will eat and sleep here at my expense; you will clothe him. What he earns after he becomes a journeyman will depend on himself."

Fu Be Be nodded. All of this was as it should be. There was, however, one small matter. "I am one person living alone. Would your guild permit my son to spend his nights in his home?"

The coppersmith thought for a moment. "It can be arranged. He must present himself daily at the Hour of the Hare and remain until his duties are finished at night."

Fu Be Be thanked him for this consideration and promised that her son's punctuality would be on her body.

"A contract!" Tang called to the accountant. When it was brought, he read the terms aloud. "Now a pen!" He turned from the clerk to Fu Be Be. "This man will sign your name for you if you will tell him what it is. Is it the Fu character for happiness or the one for a worker?"

Fu Be Be looked up timidly. "It is the character for teacher, Honorable Proprietor, and uses twelve strokes in the writing."

Tang and the clerk stared at her in amazement. "You recognize written words?" asked the coppersmith.

Young Fu watched his mother shake her head in denial. "No, I am but a stupid countrywoman, but my husband knew several tens of characters, and he taught me our name."

Her son noticed the accountant's expression change, and his body grew hot with disappointment. That his mother had been able to tell them the correct word for their name was good; if only she might have written it as well! In these people, respect for such ability was plain to see. At home there had been little talk of learning. With the earth demanding a man's entire attention, there was no time for books. Their village was too small to support a school, and if there had been one, no child could have been spared from the fields. Yes, girls perhaps might, but who would waste good money trying to educate girls?

When letters needed to be sent, the Head of the Village would draft a few crude sentences explaining the matter in hand. Sayings from the Classics, handed down from one generation to another, were a part of daily speech. And occasionally a wandering story-teller would appear at the small inn and regale those who could stay to listen with tales drawn from centuries of history. Once or twice his father had taken him to hear these romancers, but that had been before the soldiers had made life an impossible hardship. Such slight contacts had been his only ones with the knowledge to be found in books. His mind formed a swift decision: he would not remain ignorant; in some way he would learn to read and write.

When the ceremonies of contract were completed, Fu Be Be whispered to her son, "Give heed to all that you are told and say little! It is the good listener who learns well. This new master of yours is, I believe, a wise one." She finished swiftly as Tang's attention centered once more on them. "Remember the turns by which we arrived here this morning, two to the left—"

Young Fu interrupted with a nod, "I know the way," and then waited silently while his mother bowed herself out of the shop.

In the street the mist had lifted and Fu Be Be gazed on either side with interest. Her bound feet made slow progress. The flagstone pavings were loose and slippery with mire, and everywhere thoroughfares were separated by flights of steps, for Chungking climbed high on its rocky promontory above the swirling currents of the Lin and the still more treacherous Yangtze.

Today she had leisure, but work must be found for the future. In this city living costs were exorbitant. To retain the shelter of the room in Dai's tenement, she would have to pay, each moon, one half of a Szechuen silver dollar. Besides the rent, there was the problem of food for herself. She was thankful that her son would be fed by Tang. She herself could live on little. Rice and sometimes *chin-t'sai*, the cheapest of green vegetables, would satisfy her needs. Meat, except on feast days, she had learned to do without, and in brewing tea she would use fewer of the precious leaves. As for clothing, their present garments would last for some time; when they became too threadbare, she would purchase material on Thief Street, where stolen goods were offered for cheap sale, and make others.

The shops about her were busy, but most of them

employed men only. The sound of light chatter attracted her attention. Women sat in a room close by and gathered pig bristles of varying lengths into uniform bunches. Fu Be Be wondered if more workers were needed. To inquire would harm no one. She came out with the promise of work to begin the next morning. After three days of learning to sort properly, she would receive ten coppers a day for twelve hours of labor, until the Great Heat arrived. Bristles to be marketable had to be thick and wiry, and summer robbed them of these qualities. But she would not worry about that now; when the time came, some other means of livelihood would present itself.

At the coppersmith's, her son was led to the farthest room and taught his first lesson in tending the fire. This he soon discovered, though no one wished to be responsible for it, was a task of the utmost importance. The heat had to be held to an even temperature, and to do this required constant attention. Fuel was fed the small furnace regularly, and if the flame failed to respond promptly, a pair of bellows flared it into life. The workmen plied from anvils to fire, and between the moments of concentration the new apprentice studied his associates.

Five journeymen there were, and he soon connected them with their names. Tsu, an old man and second in importance to Tang, was short and his face was a network of wrinkles. His speech, though Young Fu could not hear it, kept his companions in high humor. At the anvil next him worked a sharp-featured man named Lu;

Young Fu thought he had never seen anyone so long of body. When Old Tsu happened to stand beside the other, the contrast was comic. But there was no underestimating the importance of this pair; that Tang counted on them was very evident, and the whole shop deferred to them in most matters. The accountant and his assistant apprentice conducted the store. On one of his errands to the furnace room, this boy, whom the workmen called by every epithet possible except his real name, Small Den, watched the new stoker critically.

"That you have been used to tilling the soil and nothing else, I can see," he remarked with a smirk.

Young Fu, sweating in the effort to place a glowing coal in a strategic position, made no reply. He would never care much for this fellow, he felt sure. As for the others, time would tell.

At midday rice he experienced the first taste of that torment with which a new apprentice is always greeted. Without acknowledging his presence, the men began to discuss the differences between city and country people, and the first seemed to have everything in their favor.

"Countrymen are always stupid!"

"Yes, but that can be forgiven; it is their appearance I find hardest to bear. Their heads are usually the shape of a turnip, and their hands and feet are twice the size of a normal being's."

"I, myself, could like them, if I had no nose. As it is, the odor of manure about their garments makes me hurry in the opposite direction."

"And such garments!"

"And their talk!"

One remark followed the other, and the men, with sly glances at the newcomer, agreed gravely to all that was said. Old Tsu's quips, though few in number, were more to the point than the rest, and Den, aping his elders, wagged his tongue incessantly.

Young Fu burned with shame and anger. He was aware of the sting of truth in much that they said. His trousers and short coat were made differently from theirs, and the earth language he spoke did contain words these people did not use. He himself had to listen sharply to catch all that they said. As for his appearance, he thought miserably that perhaps his head was the shape of a turnip. He would look into the next puddle he came to and find out. Hungry as he was, the hot rice stuck in his throat. He wanted nothing so much as to get back to that village which only last night he had scorned. He forced the food down his throat as Den's voice ran on; he would not let these city people see how much he suffered at their hands.

Unexpected relief came with Tang's entrance. The master sat down and told Den to bring him food. Old Tsu squinted in mock horror, "Let me bring it, please, instead of this honorable apprentice. His talk this noon has been weighted with wisdom. I had not guessed he knew so much about this business. Is it possible that you have offered him a partnership?"

Tang joined with the others in laughter, and Young Fu forgot his own wretchedness long enough to appreciate this fun at Den's expense. The talk turned abruptly to politics, and the men were soon in a hot discussion as to what would happen to Chungking if the present Tuchun should be defeated.

After a while Lu told the new apprentice to clear away the bowls. The youth collected them and carrying them to the rear room set them down on a table while he blew the fire once more to intense heat. Then pouring hot water over a dirty, gray rag he swabbed the inside of the bowls and wiped off the chopsticks. As he placed them neatly on a shelf, a boy's voice called out, "Give me a bowl! Is there rice still in the pot?"

Young Fu whirled about. This was someone he had not seen before. "There is rice in plenty," he replied.

The newcomer used his sleeve to wipe perspiration from his face. "That is good, for I am starved to death. So you are the new apprentice! What is your name?"

"Fu."

"Mine is Li." He lifted the food to his lips.

Young Fu made no effort to continue the conversation. While the newcomer assumed no superior airs, he might if opportunity arose find delight in exercising his talents along this line. The tall Lu entered and held a sheet of metal in the heat. He poised the tongs carefully and spoke: "When Small Li has eaten, you will go with him to deliver a *mei-shiang-tz* of kettles. It is too heavy for him to carry alone; also, in this fashion you will become familiar with the city."

They set out, the *mei-shiang-tz* suspended from a carrying pole, the flat ends of which rested on a shoulder of each boy. Young Fu soon learned the swinging stride which load-bearers used, and Li cleared a path for them through the crowded thoroughfares by yelling, "Open the way for a load of brasses!"

Li was shorter in stature than himself, but older. He seemed genial and inclined to ask questions.

"Where is your home?"

Young Fu hesitated. If he told, this fellow would mock him too. Then let him! He was not ashamed of his native place. "The village of Three Pools, near Tu-To," he replied sharply.

"My grandfather was a farmer," proffered his companion, "and while my father's house has lived nowhere but Chungking, we do not, of course, consider it our home. But one is safer behind strong city walls than in open fields. There, nothing checks soldiers and bandits."

"A true saying!"

"But," the other continued, "my father misses the soil. And I can understand. Once last spring we went through the land gate to the village of Dsen Gia Ngai. There were fields of rice and mustard, and, on the paths, grass. It was good to look at and very clean. Some day I hope to cross the Great River to the hills. From their highest points, it is said, one can see long distances, even to the provinces of Kweichow and Yunnan, but that naturally is on a day when the sky holds no cloud."

Young Fu warmed to this companion. They moved aside to flatten against a compound wall that two sedan chairs might pass in the narrow street. The two passengers were gentlemen of wealth and, as they recognized each other, fans were raised hurriedly before their faces in greeting. The ceremonies attendant on stopping would have required some time, and by this gesture each indicated courteously that he was in a great hurry.

The sedan chairs having passed, the boys once more swung into step. "Where do you now dwell?" asked Li.

"On Chair-Makers' Way."

"My family lives on Chicken Street, but I, of course, share the coppersmith's roof. You will sleep next me, I suppose."

"No, my mother is alone and this morning she asked the master if I might return to keep her company each night."

"That is not the custom." Small Li's eyes were wide with surprise. "But then Tang's payments to the Brass-workers' Guild are so large that it is easier for him than for most to arrange things to his own liking." He sighed. "I am sorry. Den is a poor companion. He wishes to forget he is still an apprentice and his ears are only for the men."

Young Fu thanked him for this friendly advance. He was moved to frankness. "Den, I think, will not regret my absence."

Small Li threw him a questioning glance. "So this early he vented his bitterness, did he? A member of his house, a cousin, wished to become Tang's apprentice. The coppersmith would not consider him. It was bad fortune enough to have one in his shop like Den; he did not wish a second. I myself heard him say it. Den will not soon forgive you for filling the place."

When they reentered the store late that afternoon, Young Fu felt braced to meet anything. One in this place was his friend, the others did not matter. As they appeared, Tang called out, "Did you enjoy yourselves playing about this afternoon? Or can it be that the customer has moved?"

Small Li bowed with a grin. Noticing his companion's confusion, he waited until they had reached the rear, then told him, "Tang is always like that. His tongue is sharp and his wit worse than Old Tsu's, but he does not beat his apprentices, and that is a great blessing. My cousin who works for a tanner bears scars from the bamboo's strokes—and for no reason but that he placed a skin with a tear on a pile of perfect ones."

That Tang had another side to his character, Young Fu discovered later. At dusk the coppersmith beckoned to him. "You need not remain to finish tonight. The ways of this city are new to you, and your mother will carry a heavy heart until you return. Do you know the direction to Chair-Makers' Way?" The youth nodded. "Then follow it without delay." His eyes held a kindly expression, and through the devious turns that led him home, Young Fu remembered it.

The light was still dim when he arrived at the shop next morning. Lanterns suspended from the ceiling softened the brasses to a satiny sheen, and Young Fu was held for a moment by the beauty on display. His pride increased; these objects were the work of men who had at one time started as apprentices. In time he, too, would be permitted to do something more than tend fires and run errands. Small Den's challenge broke the spell, "Did you never see a piece of brass before, countryman?"

Young Fu's countenance hardened. This morning was not yesterday! Coolly he faced his antagonist, "If I have not, is it your affair?"

"Ai!" exclaimed Den turning to the accountant for appreciation, "his temper is easily fired!"

Tang, suddenly appearing, took the conversation into his own control. "As is mine, when I see the dust still thick where you have left it."

Small Den began to whisk furiously at the offending tables, and the other boy lost no time in applying himself to the fire. Twice his enemy had lost face in his presence. This would be something to remember for future consolation. Also, his first opinion that the coppersmith missed nothing was being momentarily proved. Wherever Tang was needed at the moment, there he was to be found. No smallest detail of the work escaped him, and he gave the impression of being in all three rooms at once. There was nothing he did not know about his craft. A hint from him saved a sheet of metal from an unnecessary degree of heat; a stroke of his thumbnail hastily corrected a weak line in a design. Under his suave influence, customers whom the clerk was unable to interest would invariably buy.

When Tang was in the store, Old Tsu would chuckle: "There is no better bargainer in this city than the master. Never does he follow a patron into the street; always they tug at their moneybags before they leave this place.

I have seen his competitor, Wu, a half li from his shop trying to persuade a reluctant buyer to return and purchase." And the men would acknowledge the truth of these statements.

Tang, though he demanded the utmost in effort and artistic achievement from his workmen, held their respect. He wasted none of his suave manner on them, he was blunt and his tongue could flay like a whip, but Young Fu soon recognized the fact that the coppersmith was just in all of his dealings, and no artisan in Chungking gave better quality of work for value received.

From sunrise to nightfall, the new apprentice had no free minutes except those stolen from errands. The workrooms were a bedlam of noise—hammers beating against anvils, chisels screeching their way into designs, voices calling out, tongs clattering beside the fire. And the oven, stretching out long tongues of green and gold flame, added its contribution of soot to the blackened figures of the journeymen and recalled to Young Fu's mind pictures he had seen of the realms in which evil spirits dwell.

His thoughts of evil spirits became vividly real one afternoon as he squatted in the middle room and polished a brazier which a workman, named Dsen, had just finished. Through the doorway he watched coolies lower an open sedan chair from which a tall, strangely dressed person stepped out. The apparition sauntered into the store and Young Fu stopped his work and gazed openmouthed. It was a foreigner. In the weeks of living in Chungking, he had not yet been close to one. Occasionsionally he saw them at a distance, but they were usually so well hidden by the inquisitive crowds that always accompanied their appearance, that he still had no idea what they were like. Tang took immediate charge of the stranger, and the clerk and Den rushed about displaying goods.

Young Fu turned to the journeyman beside him. "Is that a man?"

Dsen laughed. "Truly you are from the country. Have you never seen a foreigner before?"

"Not so close. And if it is a man, even you will agree that he wears the jacket and loose trousers of a woman."

"All of their men dress in this fashion, and their women clothe their bodies in men's skirts. Everything they do is the opposite of accepted custom. The women all have feet as large as coolies', and they go about, even the young ones, in open chairs that expose their faces to the gaze of the world. The shoes they wear have thin pegs under the heels, to make them taller, I suppose, though High Heaven knows they are ungainly enough by nature. And their hair flies loosely about their faces and they laugh and talk as freely as a man. But they are as all other barbarians: they have no polite rules of conduct, and we of the Middle Kingdom can feel pity."

The boy listened attentively, but his eyes never left the figure in the store. The foreigner moved restlessly about the room, pointing out objects with a long stick and refusing to sit down and drink tea, which was what any Chinese gentleman would have done in the same circumstances.

"I like not his face," Young Fu told the journeyman. "The skin is white with bristles and resembles a poorly plucked fowl, and his nose is twice the size it should be."

Dsen went on with his work. "I felt the same about the first one I saw. When he opened his mouth to smile, he was so ugly I thought it would kill me. But I am used to them now, and while I see no good in them, I do not believe with the women that they cause bad fortune. Indeed, they are too stupid for any sensible man to fear. With money they are fools, paying coolies for every service twice what they ought to receive. But they are rich, and silver means nothing to them. They have meat every meal, it is said, and the choicest vegetables and fruit. Even the poorest among them lives like a Mandarin."

The foreigner, who showed no particular interest in the objects before him, was attempting to explain his dissatisfaction to Tang. Young Fu strained to hear, but nothing reached him above the usual uproar of the room.

"What language does he speak?" he asked Dsen.

"English, and some few words of Chinese, I suppose."

"Does Tang understand English?"

"No, but what the fellow cannot say in Chinese, the coppersmith will guess."

Tang came swiftly toward them. "With such industry in an apprentice, my fortune is made already," he remarked wryly in passing.

Old Tsu called out, "Does nothing suit your rich customer?"

"Nothing in the store. He wishes a finer piece to send

as a gift to his friend in America. He shall see the best that we have." The master moved to a large chest, pulled a key from his belt, inserted it in the triangular hanging lock, and lifted the lid.

Young Fu's hands moved rhythmically over the surface of the brazier, but stolen glances told him everything. He had noticed that chest many times but he had paid it little attention. That shopkeepers did not show their finest stock in the open store was news to him.

Tang beckoned. "Wipe your greasy hands and carry these to Den."

At the partition to the outer room, the youth halted. Fu Be Be's warnings about foreigners returned to him in full force. Suppose evil should fall on him as a result of being close to this creature. His skin prickled; then he moved forward. Evil was certain to follow if he made Tang angry by not obeying orders, and the unknown seemed the lesser of the two. He gave the articles carefully to Small Den. On his third return to the inner room, a voice called after him, "Tell your master I wish to hurry."

Startled, Young Fu glanced over his shoulder. That had been the foreigner speaking. He could not believe his own ears. He himself knew no English, so the man must have used Chinese words. In a daze he repeated the message to Tang.

"Always these foreigners must hurry," remarked the coppersmith. "They waste good time studying their

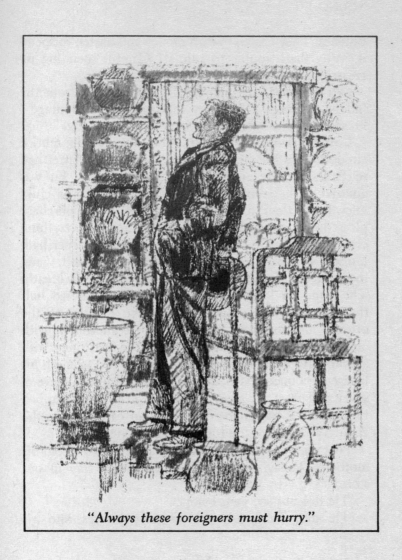

"Always these foreigners must hurry."

watches. They hasten to earn money and hasten to spend it. Why then trouble to gain it? Careful spending increases riches."

Old Tsu was now helping Tang to choose from the hidden treasures. "His hurry will be to your advantage," he said. "He will not linger over the bargaining."

Carrying a tray and a jar, Tang and the apprentice strode toward the customer. In a moment the latter had selected the tray and asked its price. Young Fu was amazed at the stupidity of such a course. Even a child knew better than to let a merchant guess which purchase pleased him most. One pretended interest in everything else and asked the price only after the storekeeper had, himself, centered attention on the article desired. Tang mentioned a sum at which Young Fu caught his breath. The foreigner looked up quizzically, then offered half the amount. Tang raised it to three fourths of the original and the other man met this compromise with one of two thirds. He accompanied the last figure with action. His hand drew from a slit in the side of his trousers—a queer place, indeed, to keep money!—several silver dollars. They were accepted. Small Den wrapped the gleaming tray in tissue paper and carried it to the chair. With a nod, the foreigner was gone.

That night on Chair-Makers' Way, Young Fu told his mother, "Today a foreign man bought a tray in our store."

"He did not see you, I hope!"

"He did. Tang told me to carry brasses into his

presence. Also, he spoke to me." At his mother's exclamation of fright, he reassured her, "Do not fear! He was ugly, but harmless."

"When did you acquire so much wisdom? Already you copy these city people. You are like a man who sits at the bottom of a well and boasts about his knowledge of the world. No one now is wise save those within the walls of the brass shop! But in the country we still know a few things, and one is that foreign barbarians should be avoided."

"But do you wish me to disobey Tang's orders?"

No reply came, and rolling in his *pu-gai,* her son fell asleep.

SERVICE AT THE POINT OF A RIFLE

AUTUMN'S SOMBER DAYS became the darker ones of winter. Rain fell daily. Fu Be Be unceasingly voiced complaints: "True, indeed, is all that I ever heard of this city's weather. In my village I believed with difficulty that rain and mist could fall anywhere without end. But so they do here. As for the sun, I see it so seldom that I jump at the sight of its rays. The very walls sweat dampness, and mildew discolors all of our possessions. To live thus is like dwelling in a grave!"

Her son grinned, "But not so lonely!"

And then, one morning there was a rift of blue in the sodden sky, and beyond the Yangtze the hills stood out in unexpected beauty of detail. Heavier rains followed, but days of glistening sunshine broke their monotony.

At Tang's the quality of weather made little difference. Trade flourished. Constantly, prospective patrons sat at the two square tables in the shop and sipped tea while Small Den ran about displaying selections suited to their demands. Young Fu and Small Li delivered orders, or, accompanied by the accountant, hurried through the streets to wealthy homes whither they had been summoned and, unwrapping their samples in the rooms reserved for trades people, awaited the buyer's pleasure. On one or two rare occasions, Tang paid these calls, but usually he trusted the business to the clerk on whose ability to get a fair price he could depend.

For Young Fu these errands were thrilling experiences. He it was who carried the heaviest brasses, he who lifted them about as the patron ordered, he who squatted on his heels in silence while the accountant pursued the delights of bargaining. He would not have exchanged positions with anyone in the Middle Kingdom. This life gave him an opportunity to see marvels that exceeded imagination.

At first he could not conceal his expressions of pleasure. "Certainly, there can be no dwellings finer than these in all the land," he said with an intake of breath.

The clerk lowered one eyelid in disdain. "When you have lived a few more years, you will not make such foolish remarks."

Young Fu said nothing more, but his opinion remained unchanged. Gatemen led them over intricate garden paths to the low, spreading buildings. Young Fu peered through carved lacquer doorways into rooms whose walls were hung with priceless scrolls and tapestries. Ebony tables and chairs, porcelain jars from which flowering trees lifted gnarled branches, tall vases a thousand years in age, vied with one another in attraction. In the spring of his ninth year, his mother had taken him to a temple several li from their farm. For a month afterwards Young Fu had been able to think of little else but the grandeur of the place. Compared with the magnificence of these homes, that of the temple now seemed on a level with his own village hut.

Sometimes it was the women of the household who wished to purchase, and the gateman would lead the tradespeople to the rear wings of the building, and there the eldest mistress of the family would receive them in the servants' gallery. Voices of younger women filtered through the thin walls, but none of these ever appeared to make their own selections. The small satin-clad and jeweled figure designated with a flourish of a tiny pipe what was desired, and in the bargaining frequently worsted Tang's representative. Young Fu, his gaze directed to the ground as was the custom in a lady's presence, found it difficult to control his amusement at such times. These old mothers, for all their wealth, differed not at all from Fu Be Be in her dealings with the shopkeepers.

Children ran along these garden paths, playing at hop-scotch with persimmon seeds for counters, or using their toes to kick a feathered shuttlecock an indefinite number of times. At one place a boy of seven was engaged in clownish antics in the effort to entertain a small girl. As the others approached, he stopped and stood in embarrassed dignity. Young Fu's glance roamed from him to the little maid. Her cheeks were streaked and her eyes red from weeping. She sat on a wooden stool and swung her feet mechanically to and fro. They were swathed in bandages that told their own story.

Girls always cried during the tedious moons of foot binding. He had seen them often enough in the village, though a few of the farm women kept their daughters' feet of natural size that they might help in the fields. But this was not common. Everyone agreed that it was better to stand the agony of foot binding than the stigma of possessing large feet. And even though deformed feet permitted a woman to work only around the house, they were important in getting a husband. Ever since that day centuries ago when an Empress had first bound her feet and then named the crippled results Golden Lilies, all of China's women had followed the fashion. He, Young Fu, was glad that his mother's feet were small; that she was not a coolie woman was plain for all to see.

In some of the homes they would find teachers instructing the boys of the family in the Classics. Sometimes these youths attended private schools in the city. Small, ill-lighted rooms set between shops on busy thoroughfares and presided over by one venerable scholar, they offered much the same subject matter and methods that they had used two thousand years before. A hundred feet away, one could determine their location. At the top of their lungs, students memorized and recited lessons, and the noise rose in waves above the other sounds of the street. Young Fu wondered at times what it would be like to have time in which to do nothing but study and play. He did not envy them, but neither did he forget that he had set himself the task some day of learning to read and write characters. It did not occur to him to tell Wang Scholar, whom he met on the curb each evening, that he wished to do books. An apprentice did not trouble a gentleman with such small affairs. Moreover, it was his duty just now to learn all that he could of Tang's business; the other would come in time.

Six months of this life had slipped by when he awoke to the realization that Chungking was not made up of magnificence and entertainment alone. On his way home at dusk one day, he noticed a crowd collected in the hollow space made by an abrupt angle of two compound walls, so built that evil spirits, which are able to travel only in a straight line, might butt themselves against this sudden obstruction and have an untimely end. Everyone knows that devils are stupid and that simple expedients like these often save a whole family from disaster. As he came nearer, the crowd dispersed. Most of them wore frightened faces, and some muttered ominously to one another. Alive with curiosity, he pressed on and found himself almost alone with a half-dozen soldiers.

In their midst was a load-coolie, his back pressed to the wall, his breast pinned by the muzzle of a rifle. His face was ashen as he attempted to reason with his persecutors.

One of the soldiers interrupted him. "I will count ten," he said. "If by that time you still refuse to carry our bedding—" he smiled cruelly.

"I dare not, Honorable Military," wailed the coolie. "I am late with my load for my master. If you do not let me hurry on, he will give me less than my due in payment, and already my family starves for lack of food."

Young Fu's gaze shifted from the miserable man to the paving. There were several bundles of bedding belonging to the soldiers, and close by sat two round baskets filled with rice, on the top of which rested the coolie's carrying pole and ropes.

"One, two, three, four, five," counted the soldier.

The coolie's face was contorted with fear. "Sirs," he begged.

"Six, seven, eight, nine, ten!"

"Sirs! What will you do—" There was a deafening report and the load-bearer's last protest died away in a faint scream. He slid silently to the ground.

Stricken with horror, Young Fu stared at the bundle of reddening rags that only a few seconds earlier had been a man intent on earning food for himself and family. The youth felt suddenly cold; he began to tremble. He wished for nothing save to escape from this revolting scene of violence, but his feet refused to move.

The soldiers were now quarreling over the deed; each blamed the other for the man's death; one in particular seemed worried. He kept murmuring that this had not been necessary, that their captain must not hear of the matter.

He who had done the shooting sneered, "Of what importance is a coolie?"

A coolie, an eating-bitterness man as he was called— what did he matter? The question burned into the youth's numbed mind. But the man had done nothing except to refuse to carry bedding that belonged to these soldiers. He had been delivering rice for his master, and because he would not leave that in the street and take up this bedding, he had been killed.

Young Fu puzzled over the injustice of the affair. And the soldiers would go unpunished; no one was ever strong enough to punish the military. First they had killed his father by destroying the crops; that had taken several years of exposure and overwork. Now this man had paid with his life, and in less than a minute of time. And if he did not slip away before they awoke to the knowledge of his presence, they might shoot him, also. He took one step when a heavy hand gripped his shoulder.

"What are you doing here?" a gruff voice demanded.

Young Fu winced in terror. "Nothing," he stammered.

"Let the boy go!" commanded the one with the worried expression.

"No," was the reply, "he looks strong. We shall, until we find help elsewhere, have to carry our bedding, but he can bring this fellow's load of rice. We can use that to good advantage."

The youth listened in a daze. He could not carry that rice. It must weigh twice as much as any of the brasses Tang had taxed his strength with, and his muscles had strained under them. "I have not the strength for this," he began, "perhaps, the bedding—"

"Do you wish to be the second to lie there?" The soldier pointed to the body.

Shivering, the boy stooped down, caught up the dead man's pole, slipped the ropes over each end, and tried to lift the baskets clear of the ground. The pole cut into his shoulders and he staggered under the painful pressure. With the unexpected jolting, a small shower of rice slid from the surface of each basket. His tormentor cursed, struck him across the back with his rifle butt, and dared him to be so careless again.

The worried man interfered, and a bitter quarrel ensued. The others shrugged their shoulders, then cautioning haste, picked up rolls of bedding and started on down the street. Young Fu, hedged in between the brawling men and the grain baskets, sought desperately for a way of escape, but there was none. Behind the basket rose the stone wall; blocking him in front were the two soldiers. He turned hopelessly to the load.

As he did so, the worried one shook his head,

Shivering, the boy stooped down . . .

motioned for his antagonist to have his way in the argument, and reached for a roll of bedding. Marshaling every ounce of strength in his young body, the boy at last managed to lift the load from the ground, and the three followed in the path of the others.

Darkness was softening the outlines of the street. It covered from curious eyes a pitiful bundle of rags which lay quietly in the hollow space made by the right angle of two compound walls. The body within the rags would not again handle a load-pole; as for its family— they would have to find some other way of earning rice. Chungking's great wealth did not prevent most of her inhabitants from living always on the verge of starvation.

To the fourteen-year-old boy now attempting to carry the load which the dead man had laid down, each movement was torture. Sweat poured from him, and his heart responded with increasingly painful thuds. Every few paces he was compelled to halt, release his neck for the moment from the weight, and fill his exhausted lungs. Shop fronts were closed and the streets almost deserted. If it were day, he might appeal for help, though this was a small hope. Who in this city, however kind of heart, would consider him of sufficient importance to risk a quarrel with soldiers about him? Dully he went on, moving more slowly each moment. At last, the soldier ordered him to stop, and bowing over his load for this brief respite, Young Fu waited for the next word.

A loud guffaw roused him to the presence of others. He looked up to see soldiers all about him. They filled a whole section of shops, sitting about tables eating, gambling, loud in discussion. He had heard that the army had quarters in one end of the city, but he had not seen them for himself. He was seeing them now and, perhaps, for the last time, for they would surely kill him —if not by rifle, then by forcing him to bear burdens like this one.

Several men rose and moved closer. There was more harsh laughter followed by speech. "Lin steals the newborn from their mothers to carry grain for him!"

"Where did you find that rice?"

"Look, the babe faints by the load!"

Young Fu struggled to command his senses. His head was whirling.

"What shall I do with him?" asked Lin, now surly over the amusement at his expense.

"Do with him? Send him away. Do you think our captain would let you keep him here for your slave? A year ago, perhaps, but now he wishes to win the favor of the new government at Nanking, and they have foolish ideas about children and law-abiding citizens. Law-abiding citizens! If I had my way, these greedy Chungkingese would be relieved of some of their treasure. Such food as they give—they would starve their defenders!" The speaker sifted rice through his fingers. "This is good grain you have brought in, Lin. Where did you get it?"

"From a grain merchant, naturally."

The youth, strength flowing back into his veins,

seethed with indignation. He did not care if they killed him, he would tell where this liar had found the rice. He opened his lips to speak, but a hand pulled him swiftly to one side. In the shadow of a neighboring door-post, the worried one, who had remained silent throughout this conversation, ordered sharply: "Close your mouth, young fool! I saw what you would do. Do you think it matters to my companions that a coolie died? Or that they would not kill you, if they wished? And had you spoken, your life would have paid for it. They would have feared the tale might later reach the captain, who desires a good name in this city and, in time, Nanking. Run, and run swiftly, before they realize that you are gone!"

For a second Young Fu stood where he was. "Why do you do this for me? Your heart is good!"

The other cursed the delay and pushed the boy along, "Because, fool, I was your age when they tore me from my father's house!" He watched the youth disappear, then stealing quietly away from Lin and the circle about him, he joined a group of soldiers several doors down the street.

After a weary hour of stumbling about unfamiliar thoroughfares, Young Fu found himself once more on Chair-Makers' Way. Before the doorway to Dai's house stood Fu Be Be and Wang Scholar. His mother was crying openly, and the old gentleman greeted him with grave concern. "Thy mother carries a heavy heart," he chided.

"Where have you been?" demanded Fu Be Be.

Her son sank down on the sill. "It was not my fault," he offered by way of explanation, and could say nothing more. He felt deathly sick. He rested his head on his arms and shook with chill.

Fu Be Be hovered above him. "Where is your pain?"

"A bowl of hot tea is what he needs now," suggested the scholar. "Later, he will be able to tell you what happened."

The mother rushed within and returned with the bowl of steaming liquid. Young Fu gulped it down. After a time he ceased shaking and Wang Scholar, aware that he could be of no further assistance, went to his room. In their own quarters the boy told the story. Fu Be Be wept.

When her son was safe in bed, she went through the doorway and down the street to a small, bare space where there was erected a shrine to Kwan Yin, the Goddess of Mercy. On the pungent, gray curls of smoke that ascended from lighted incense, she offered her gratitude to the kindly looking little statue within. In the future she must remember to be more faithful about these offices; experiences such as her son had known this night were common to a great city. How she disliked the place with its crowds and noise!

As for her work with the bristles! She caught her breath. She must not be ungrateful. Her work meant food. And her son was learning fast. The more she heard of his master, Tang, the better satisfied she was about the apprenticeship. And her own unpleasant work was a small affair when she remembered from what grave danger her son had just been saved. She stopped in the middle of the road; she had neglected to ask Kwan Yin's special protection for that soldier. Hastily she retraced her steps to the shrine.

"IF A MAN'S AFFAIRS ARE TO PROSPER"

WEEKS PASSED before Young Fu felt a sense of security on the streets. At dawn he walked with his mother as far as the bristle shop, and though he was only too glad for the comfort of a companion, he would have bitten his tongue before admitting to Fu Be Be either his fear or his dependence on her. At dusk he mingled as inconspicuously as possible in the milling throngs of the Chungking streets. Curiosity, which prior to his experience with the soldiers had controlled most of his actions, was now severely tempered by the determination to avoid like dangers in the future. The sight of a single soldier sitting in a tea house was sufficient to quicken his normal pace into a run. Small Li, on one of their ceaseless errands, noticed his friend's aversion to a gray uniform, and questioned him. "Why are you so afraid of the military? I myself do not get in their way, but you avoid them as you would an evil spirit."

Young Fu evaded the reply. So vivid was his memory of the horror, that he could not bring himself to relate it again. A day after it had occurred he had told Wang Scholar who had listened in silence save for sympathetic clicks of the tongue and one comment at the close, "Good iron is not wasted in making nails, nor good men in making soldiers!"

At Tang's, the workmen, discussing political conditions, as usual, over the midday rice, said that these troops were behaving better than most; at least, general looting was not taking place and, so far, a very moderate tax had been levied.

"The fewer words about such things, the better," remarked Tang. "It has been my experience that Tuchuns are all alike in their greed for money and power. Sometimes their methods differ. If this one seems to be dealing gently with us now, then there is greater reason to expect rough handling in the future."

This warning served to change the apprentice's skin

to goose flesh, but as the weeks lengthened into months and the city relaxed in continued quiet, his heart grew braver, and he began to run about with his old freedom.

There was little he did not know by this time of Chungking's lanes and byways. Tang's errands sent him in every direction, from one city gate to another. He knew at what hour a storyteller would be likely to stand at a certain angle of wall and thrill his audience with tales from history. He could tell where one might expect to find, each tenth day of the moon, a peep show stationed—one with puppets of remarkable gifts. His nose scented funeral and wedding processions, and whenever possible, he directed his errands according to these various attractions.

Each forenoon a public letter writer sat before one of the foreign temples (a French cathedral) and almost daily Young Fu made it his business to halt for a moment that he might watch the other draw the strokes of characters. Already he had memorized some of the simpler ones. Given time, he would learn more. Small Li, who had now become his close friend, did not share his comrade's enthusiasm for stolen knowledge.

"I, too, wish to learn," he said, "but not with this load swinging from my shoulders. Moreover, while I do not fear the master's sharp tongue too greatly, it is wise not to provoke him by constant tardiness."

Young Fu waved an open palm in inquiry, "How then is one ever to learn? And you yourself told me not to be afraid of the coppersmith's scoldings."

Small Li said nothing further. Several hours later Wang Scholar reopened this conversation. He came upon Young Fu as the boy, forefinger extended, penciled shadowy lines on the darkness of Chair-Makers' Way. The teacher looked on with interest.

"Who taught you to write the word for door with seven strokes?"

"I watched the letter writer before the foreign temple. That and other words have I learned," the student boasted with pride.

"Then learn something more: 'There is no merit worthy of boasting!' And thine of this newly acquired knowledge, less than most, for the strokes were wrong."

Young Fu was crestfallen. "My heart is hot with shame, Honorable One, but I thought by studying this letter writer I might discover how to read and write."

"It is better to remain ignorant than to know what is incorrect. Come with me!" he commanded, and the youth followed him up the ladder to the second floor.

He had not gone there before, though he had wished to do so many times. Fu Be Be had cautioned him about intruding on the thinker's privacy. The furnishings of the room were of the simplest kind, poorer even than his mother's, but books were in profusion. He gazed at them reverently. "Sir, you are very rich!"

Wang Scholar smiled and nodded his head. "Poor and unworthy am I," he agreed, "but here is the wealth of the ages." He motioned for the boy to sit at the table, and joining him took up the brush-pen. This he moistened, rolled the hairs into a fine point on the slab of ink, and, pulling a thin, yellow sheet of paper toward him, began to write.

"Learn, as should any good student, the first sentence from the San-Tz-Ching: 'At birth, men are by nature good of heart.' "

Fascinated, his pupil watched. With flushed cheeks he received the brush from the teacher and copied the characters as best he could. Wang Scholar mingled words of encouragement and chiding. When he decided that the boy had done enough for one night, he drew the writing materials toward him. "In time thou wilt learn to form the strokes with ease. Patience and industry are all that is required of the student." He studied Young Fu's expression. "Why dost thou wish to do books?"

The other hesitated for a moment. "I do not know," he replied. "Since the day I first became apprenticed to Tang, I have wanted to recognize characters and write them. In this city it is necessary to have learning in order to win fortune. He who can read and write is not so easily cheated of his rights." He looked up to find the old gentleman's face stern with disapproval.

"And is there no other reason?" Wang Scholar demanded. "Shall I teach the Ancient Wisdom to one who wishes to use it only for the earning of money? Knowest thou not that the treasure of knowledge is to be revered for itself alone? It has been given that men might learn how to live, not to win fortune. What is fortune without wisdom?" His voice slowly resumed its

"What is fortune without wisdom?"

even tone. "Thou art young, and I who am old forget the dreams of youth. Go now and return to me tomorrow night. Together we shall study what the sages have taught."

Young Fu crept slowly down the stairs. In the doorway, he looked on the sleeping street. Wisdom had been given that men might learn how to live. This was a new doctrine, indeed. And certain it was that Chungking City, as he saw it from daylight to dark, heeded little but the importance of earning money. Was this why scholars seemed different from other people? Puzzled, he entered the house.

"Where have you been so late?" his mother wished to know.

"In Wang Scholar's room. Tonight he taught me my first lessons, and I go to him again tomorrow at this hour."

Fu Be Be blinked tired eyelids. "Ai!" she exclaimed, "this is a great business! Where will you find money to pay a teacher?"

Her son dismissed the matter with a wave of the hand. "None is needed. Tonight Wang Scholar told me that money was of small importance."

Fu Be Be opened her eyes more widely to stare at him, then closed them and yawned. "Hurry," she ordered, "or we shall be rising before we have slept."

In the days following, Young Fu made no effort to pass the letter writer's stand. Once Small Li questioned him about his loss of interest. It was on the tip of his companion's tongue to speak of his good fortune in having a real teacher, but he did not. As yet he knew very little. Each evening Wang Scholar made him sense more clearly the boundless reaches of learning, and it would be wise to have a foundation before his associates at Tang's put his scholarship to the test, as he knew only too well they were capable of doing. Few of them could name more than a handful of characters; some, none at all; Tang and the clerk had the widest information out of books. And, as for the latter, Young Fu had his doubts about how far his attainments extended. There was not one among the older employees he liked so little as he did this man. Just why he could not say. In some inexplicable way the accountant was connected with his feeling against Small Den, perhaps because the older man wore constantly the supercilious air that Den strove so hard to copy.

But most clerks were like that. Reckoning accounts on the abacus and writing the results in books made them feel vastly superior to the journeymen and apprentices with whom they associated. Also, they were accustomed to having others do all unpleasant tasks for them. He, who had accompanied this one on the errands to wealthy homes, knew that only too well. And he would not now give the fellow the pleasure of laughing over the idea of an apprentice turned student. He wished, though, that he might tell Li—they were friends; but if he did, the whole shop would know it by midday. Li was not very successful about hiding things in his brain.

One afternoon Tang called him. He held a letter.

"Take this," he said, "to Beh Carpenter who lives mid-
way on the road between the Land Gate and the village,
Dsen-Gia-Ngai. The captain on a foreign gunboat wishes
a small table of teakwood with a brass tray fitted in the
top. He must have it within two days, before he sails
down the Great River. If Beh Carpenter cannot complete the table in that time, I wish to know at once."

Young Fu turned his steps toward the Land Gate. In
a clearing before a sugar-manufacturer's place he halted
to watch an ox turn a treadmill. Steadily the patient
beast plodded the circle, moving the great, flat stone
that crushed the sweetened juice from cane stalks.
Round and round it went in endless revolutions. The
boy wondered how the animal could continue hour after
hour; his own head felt dizzy from watching.

Passing through the city gate, his pace quickened
down the Dsen-Gia-Ngai road. Beggars were as thick
as flies. Every conceivable disease and deformity of body
had its victim here. Many for the sake of business bore
self-inflicted wounds. Others had been crippled for that
purpose in early youth by parents in the same profession.
One could not remain in the Beggars' Guild and present
a normal body to the world. And since it was much
simpler to earn a livelihood by asking alms than by
laboring like a coolie, many chose that way and wore
without question its disfiguring symbols.

In the city, beggars whining about a shop could ruin
a merchant's trade and, in order to relieve themselves
of this nuisance, most shopkeepers paid a regular tax to
be exempt from their annoyance. Others there were, of

course, sad outcasts of illness and poverty, who had been forced into this life of wretchedness.

Traffic at this hour of the day was heavy, and they paid little attention to a boy whose discolored garments and stained hands marked him as an apprentice. Sedan chairs and more-prosperous-looking travelers were their natural prey and each, in turn, was forced to run the awful gauntlet of their demands for charity. "Pity me! You have food, clothing, a home. I starve in rags; this stone is my bed. Of your wealth give me a copper! Only a copper! Only a copper!"

Young Fu soon left them behind. He began to take delight in the scene about him. The country road was rough and winding, but on either side lay richly fertile fields. His thoughts winged back to the little farm near Tu-To and the days spent with his father as they cultivated the crops. Within him was a strange feeling of discomfort and emptiness. Almost a year had passed since his father's death, but the realization of his loss came to him, at this moment, with greater force than ever before.

Certainly, he told himself, he was growing older. That he could lift heavier weights, he knew. And that his blue cotton clothes never seemed long enough to reach his wrists and ankles, was true, also. Pity for that man who had worked so hard and reaped so little swept over him. His father had been good. His shoulders straightened at the memory. He himself was the only son of his house. He would see to it that his ancestors had no cause to be ashamed of his actions!

Beh Carpenter's shop was sheltered by willows that rose above a pool. The afternoon sun filtered through the leaves and spattered lacy patterns on the earthen floor of the workroom. Men sawed at a great log, and the sweet odor of green wood filled the nostrils. On the floor three children played with sawdust and shavings. While the proprietor read Tang's note, Young Fu picked up a curl and tickled the bare shoulders of a small boy. The youngster darted out of his reach and continued his play. There was an air of peace about this workshop very different from the clamor and smoke of the copper-smith's place.

Beh Carpenter hesitated over the reply. "Two days means holding back other orders, but I suppose it might be arranged." He wrote a few characters and gave the paper to the youth.

Sunset was mellowing all that it touched when the Land Gate again came into view. From either direction people hurried through this entrance to the city. At dark the great doors would be barred, permitting no one to go in or out until dawn lightened the eastern sky. A handsome sedan chair demanded the right of way, and Young Fu stepped aside. The beggars swarmed about it, blocking the path of its bearers as they whined their pleas for pity. That the occupant had no time to waste, was plain. Without warning, a wire strung with fifty cash hurtled through the air, struck one of the beggars clinging to the chair poles, and landed in the withered arms of a leper close to Young Fu's feet. The wretched horde, startled by the unexpectedness of the gift, turned from the chair, as its bearers moved stolidly on, and sniffed like dogs who have lost a trail. In another moment they had swooped in a mass on the unhappy recipient of the treasure.

Young Fu watched in disgust. The leper drew his wasted limbs together and huddled protectingly over his sudden stroke of good fortune, as his hideous companions, flapping bundles of filth and tatters, screamed imprecations on his head and turned their crutches into weapons with which to pry him loose from the coins. Aroused by the unusual tumult, a soldier ran down from the gate and prodding indiscriminately with his rifle, succeeded in separating the mob. The leper was still alive, but he no longer held anything of value. Near him, a man who wore a thin knife blade through the fleshy part of his wrist from which drops of blood oozed slowly—a never-failing method of gaining pity—made a suspicious movement. Instantly the beggars' attention centered on him.

"Curse him! He has it! He would steal what belongs to all! Divide! Divide!" they yelled, "or we will take the matter to the king (the head of the Beggars' Guild)!"

The soldier demanded the booty. "Who caught this when it fell?"

"I! I! I!" screeched one after the other. From the panting bundle on the ground a faint moan issued. The soldier looked about; his glance discovered Young Fu. "Did you see?" he asked.

The apprentice found it difficult to speak. Fear of questioning by soldiers was still fresh in his mind. He motioned with his chin to the leper and as soon as the other's gaze left him, he made for the gate. Over his shoulder he was aware that the rightful owner again held the cash. How long they would remain in his possession now that night was approaching was another problem. The soldier was attempting to quiet the thwarted group; some had already resumed business. As he climbed the slope to the city, stumbling steps sounded behind him. He looked back. The man with the knife in his wrist hissed at him, "If you had not told, the money would have been ours to share. When you come this way again, we will remember!"

With a shrug, Young Fu passed into the city. A beggar's threat meant little. Pleading and cursing were the limits of their language. He had felt much greater fear when that soldier first turned to him. And for having loitered so long, he now had Tang's annoyance to face. He began to run.

Three moons went by before the youth had cause to remember the beggar's warning—three months of a growing friendship for Small Li, an increasing antipathy for Den, an ever greater respect for Tang. He was learning all of the small details of the business. Dsen had given him the first lesson in welding; he was ambitious for the hour when Old Tsu or the tall Lu would teach him more. At night, wearied as he was from the day's toil, he climbed the steps to Wang Scholar's room and studied some saying from the Classics. He could now recognize more than a hundred characters, and for one whose hands were roughened and enlarged by manual labor, his writing was not bad, to judge from Wang Scholar's encouraging remarks.

Fu Be Be was delighted with his progress, but weighed down with the sense of obligation to the teacher. She was in no position to make gifts of money or anything else of value, and the realization of what Wang Scholar was doing toward her son's future advancement made her grasp at opportunities of service. During the period of Great Heat, her work at the bristle shop was discontinued and she was unable to find other employment. In the free weeks that followed she took upon herself the task of mending the old gentleman's garments. Once on a feast day, when her son was at home for the meal, she prepared sweetened eggs and sent a share of the delicacy to the upper room. In such small ways she not only eased her own mind, but added greatly to Wang Scholar's physical comfort as well.

Her work, to which she returned with the arrival of cool weather, was no longer so trying as she had first found it, though she still looked forward to the day when her son would be a journeyman, earning a living for the two of them. The boy was hard for her to understand. Sometimes his actions seemed foolish beyond all imagination, but the coppersmith had told her he was satisfied, and Wang Scholar credited the youth with a student's brains. If these wise persons knew no fear for her son's future, she could rest her heart.

It was fortunate she did not go through his days with him, or she might not have been so easily set at peace. Swinging through the Land Gate with a finely cut brazier

which Beh Carpenter was giving to a friend, Young Fu
repeated the sentence he had learned the preceding night
and formed the words, stroke by stroke, in his mind's eye,
"If a man's affairs are to prosper, it is simply a matter of
purpose." His thoughts ran in and out between the characters. "Simply a matter of purpose!" True, indeed! He
had determined to learn books, and lo! Wang Scholar
had invited him to study.

He was trying to think of another illustration of the
maxim to his own credit, when he tripped, fell headlong
over an extended stick, and saw the brazier go bouncing
from rut to rut and roll into a ditch. As he picked up his
bruised body, harsh cackles of laughter echoed in his
ears, but he did not stop to identify them. The brazier
was his one concern; even if the soft tissue still protected
the surface, it was sure to be dented from the hard
knocks it had received. Several beggars reached the ditch
before he did. Dancing about, their faces distorted in
ghoulish glee, they stretched the gleaming object above
the boy's reach.

"Whose is it? Whose is it? Whose is it?" they taunted.
"You knew whose the cash were! Now tell us is the
brazier yours or ours?"

Anger rushed to Young Fu's head. He snatched at
the nearest crutch and used it like a flail. "Give it to
me!" he ordered.

His tormentors bowed under the sudden onslaught.
"Give it to the rotten egg, or he will kill us!" The tallest
pulled a knife from his belt, drew a number of hasty

scratches over the surface and hurled the brazier far down the road.

Young Fu raced after it. He lifted it carefully, wiped off the dust and stared. His heart sank like a stone. Dents were everywhere and over all the tearing, jagged scratches. Beh Carpenter would never accept this. And if that were true, how could he return to the coppersmith? What excuse was there to offer? That he had been innocent in the affair he knew, but if he had not been lost in boasting to himself of his achievements, he might have remembered this spot and been on guard for trouble. To tell Tang that beggars had deliberately tripped him would not satisfy that keen-witted gentleman. Beggars were troublesome, but usually they stuck to their business. Tang would scent a past to justify such action on their part. And when he admitted to the first meeting and the loitering that had embroiled him in it, what would Tang say to that?

He might, something told him, go on to Beh Carpenter's shop and, avoiding the proprietor, leave it with someone else, on whom the blame for scarring might fall. Perhaps, if he found the children playing about he might see to their dropping it. "Ai!" What was he, he asked himself angrily, to make the innocent suffer for his fault? He hugged the object to him, and, waiting for an auspicious moment when heavy traffic was bound for Chungking, he slipped again into the city.

Toward the coppersmith's shop Young Fu pursued a circuitous path, delaying as long as possible the inevitable confession. Attractions that would have intrigued his lively curiosity under ordinary conditions passed unseen; his very soul was crushed beneath the weight of the battered brazier.

As he neared the shop, his steps grew steadily slower. What Tang would do, he had no idea, but that his punishment would be heavy was certain. He dragged his feet over the door sill. Den grinned and flung at him a taunting remark about his unexpected return; Young Fu let it pass unnoticed. To his good fortune, Tang was in the furnace room, and he went directly to him.

The coppersmith looked up surprised, "Why are you back this early?" Then as his eyes lighted on the piece of brass, he inquired sharply, "What has happened?"

"I have ruined Beh Carpenter's brazier."

"What?" He snatched the article from the boy's hands. "And you dare to tell me this?"

Frightened and miserable, Young Fu murmured, "I did not know what else to do."

Tang's curiosity overcame his first wave of anger. Perhaps there was more to this than lay on the surface. He pushed the apprentice to a corner of the room and demanded an explanation.

Young Fu told what had just occurred. As he had expected, the master interrupted to ask, "What had you done to make them your enemies?"

The earlier circumstance was related.

"But why did the soldier ask you and not some other?"

Young Fu was conscious of the trap even as he answered, "I saw the whole affair."

"So you were the only one on the road that day with leisure to spend on so unimportant a matter, is it not so? That you waste my time constantly on errands is of more loss to me than several braziers."

Young Fu's unhappy gaze sought the floor. He had thought it clever before to enjoy himself on Tang's errands, but now! "I did not think," he offered apologetically.

"It is not the custom of youth to do so," the coppersmith responded wryly. "Learn this for the future when you would give your attention to what is unimportant: 'If a man's affairs are to prosper, it is simply a matter of purpose!' "

Young Fu reddened afresh at this quotation. The memory of his earlier boasting stung him. He stood waiting for the next move, but the master seemed to have forgotten his presence. Tang was smoothing the disfigured brazier with tender touch. Suddenly he looked up, "Is there nothing to be done in this place? Get to work!"

The boy gasped in astonishment. "Is that all?" he stammered.

"Would it make this brazier new if I beat you? Punishment, though, you shall bear. For the rest of this moon, Small Li shall do all of the errands. Here, close to the shop, you may learn the value of time. Waste no more of it! At this moment the fire needs attention. Ai! would that the gods might sometime send me an apprentice that was worth his food!" He moved from the room, carrying the brazier with him, and Young Fu, still dazed by all that had befallen, caught up the bellows and blew the flame furiously into action.

This punishment, though a deprivation, was far less than he had expected, or, as he told himself, had deserved. It was not he but Tang who was paying most dearly for his affair. An expensive piece of work had been ruined, and, according to the coppersmith, the loss of the brazier did not compare with that of the hours that had been wasted in loitering. He was suddenly ashamed. As Tang's apprentice, he was having an opportunity that many a Chungking youth craved. He was a part of this establishment, and what affected Tang, in turn affected him. This was a new idea, but he would not soon forget it. With a deft twist of the tongs the penitent apprentice rescued a piece of charcoal from the side of the oven and placed it where it would contribute its full flame to the fire.

FOR SALE — DRAGON'S BREATH, CHEAP

EACH DAY that remained to the month was one of torment. Young Fu was not certain how much Tang had told the journeymen about the brazier, but an occasional coupling of his name with the word beggar made him suspicious. His constant presence in the workroom was sufficient explanation to Den that the new apprentice was in disgrace, and no opportunity was lost to remind him of it. True to his word, with the appearance of a new moon, Tang once more sent him outside. The regained freedom was so delightful that Young Fu finished his errands as if by magic.

Small Li, when they were on trips together, complained about the unnecessary speed. "Before your trouble you used more time than I on the coppersmith's business; now you go as though a *ya-men* runner searched for you."

His companion slowed down a little. He would not soon forget the lesson he had learned, but there was no need to run Li breathless. Even Tang complimented him on the dispatch with which he now accomplished matters. These remarks were tinged with the customary sarcasm, but Young Fu sensed the appreciation of improvement that lay beneath.

A year and more had he served of his apprenticeship; a year and still more remained. By New Year's the period would reach an even half. Time would fly and he would become a journeyman earning good silver for himself and Fu Be Be. She might then cease working at the bristle shop, for he would take good care of her. He had, he believed, a head above most of the other artisans. They still made fun of his welding, and Old Tsu raised hands in horror over his attempts to design, but in time he would let them see. One thing he knew—he could read more characters than any save Tang and the accountant.

In the weeks that followed, life moved smoothly

along an even groove. Once or twice Old Tsu commented favorably on one of Young Fu's designs, and the boy's satisfaction grew apace. Was this not a proof of the ability with which he credited himself? And then, with the unexpectedness of a lightning stroke, this small world of self-confidence that he had been building crumbled into ruins at his feet.

One evening, as Young Fu returned early from the last errand of the day, Tang dismissed him with the suggestion that he go play a little. Surprise at this unexpected freedom held the apprentice motionless for a moment, then he folded his leather apron, laid it away, and passed into the street. For lack of something more exciting to do, he directed his steps toward Thief Street. The stolen goods, displayed there on the open stalls, offered nothing of unusual interest, and it was not until he had turned into one of the larger business thoroughfares that evil fortune gripped him.

There, in a jeweler's shop, hung a shining, nickel watch, large and round and, strange to say, black of face. Young Fu had seen several watches in his lifetime, but never one with a dark face. He stopped and studied it. Then, following his fate, he had crossed the sill and asked the proprietor to tell him the reason for such a color.

Hsui, the jeweler, was stout and prosperous, with all of the tricks of the trade at his command. "I do not recognize you," he began, "but you are a young man of very great acumen. That valuable treasure has been hanging there on display for three days, and you are the first with sufficient intellect to note its extraordinary appearance."

This opening at once knocked down all the defenses which the youth might normally have had in the presence of a shopkeeper. He was used to remarks of another color. Open-mouthed he stared into Hsui's face, charmed by this sudden acceptance of his own feelings about himself. In a daze he watched Hsui take down the watch and then beckon him to a dark corner of the shop. Right there, Young Fu was given one of the greatest shocks of his life. Held in the darkness, the watch glowed into a live thing, and the figures upon its face turned before his eyes into so many tiny snakes of fire. He felt cold all over, but now that another thought of him so highly, he concealed his trembling and mumbled only in a shaky voice, "*Shi chi deh hun* (extremely queer)!"

Hsui, fully aware of his victim's state of mind, pursued the game. "And only you, of all the people in Chungking, knew what to expect of this gift for an emperor. You must, indeed, be a much traveled man and a learned one, for truly this is the first time that anything of the sort has been shown in this great city."

Young Fu was almost overcome with delight. The hypnotizing voice droned on: "Let me press this gift upon you. I can sleep without dreams if I know that it is in your possession. A sacrifice for me, yes, a great one—but then to meet with one of your intelligence is a rare privilege, and I am willing to pay for the experience!"

"Do you mean to give me this precious gift?" asked Young Fu.

"Just that," insisted Hsui, "just that! You may take the watch with you now. I ask only one small favor: that you sign this bit of paper which my neighbor, Liu, will witness, and sometime when fortune is yours, send me the paltry sum of five dollars, as an acknowledgment of the gift."

The neighbor appeared as if by magic, and before the youth could catch his breath, he found himself on his homeward way, with the watch in his hand.

His pleasure in the newly acquired treasure soon faded. To begin with, Fu Be Be was horrified at the debt of five dollars. "We shall have to beg on the streets, or starve!" she wailed. "I shall have no coffin for a decent burial!" At this last thought, tears took the place of words. For the ruling desire of her life was to save enough from their income to purchase her coffin. She had dreamed of its presence in this wretched room of Dai's, a sweet-smelling wooden box to be used as table and chest until the day when she herself would occupy it in state. Now all of her hopes lay about her. Her son earned nothing, and she very little. A debt of five dollars was something not to be faced and all because this stupid boy had shown no more sense than to buy this "foreign devil's" machine. "What do we need of a watch?" she demanded shrilly. "When I wish to know the hour, I can look in the eyes of my neighbor's cat and find out."

Defenseless against this blame, Young Fu blew out the

candlelight suddenly and showed her the watch in the dark. Fu Be Be shrieked. "It is some foreign devil's spirit come to live with us and disgrace my old age! What have I done that I should have a son so brainless?"

In the period that followed, Young Fu returned each evening to face these same questions and others of like nature. He went forth each morning to be accosted by Hsui or his clerk concerning the little matter of the five dollars and the "bit of paper." Under the combined torments he grew thin. Flown was his sense of wisdom and self-importance; he knew now that never in the history of the house of Fu had there been such a dolt as himself.

And then, as if he were not already miserable enough, the watch lost its power to charm. Originally it had cost somewhere in America the sum of ninety-eight cents; it had come a long way from home and was tired. One morning in the second month of his possession, its main-spring gasped in a final effort and all of its contents settled into peaceful relaxation. A few days later, unable to adapt themselves to Chungking's uncertain climate, the small, fiery snakes grew paler and paler until darkness and light became one and the same thing.

"No good! It was worn out when I got it," growled Young Fu to himself disgustedly. But for the first time in weeks Fu Be Be smiled. Within her was the assurance that the incense and rice which she had placed before Kwan Yin's shrine had achieved the foreign spirit's death, and her scoldings lost some of their sting.

With her assistance, two dollars had been paid to

Hsui, but now the New Year was upon them and the balance was still owing. Fu Be Be refused to let him have anything from her small store of savings for this festival; better to owe a debt to man than to cheat the gods of their offerings. "That would only mean more trouble for the coming year," she told him, "and who can say but that your actions have already placed us in disfavor with heavenly authority?"

The night on which the kitchen god left for the spirit world with his report (a week before the New Year dawned) she had, due to this very fear, added to the usual oblation of sweetmeats a few drops of wine in the hope that his statement of affairs in this household might be less clearly rendered. This year, above all others, would she see to it that the gods had their due.

"But Hsui—" stammered her son, "Hsui must be paid. One day only remains before the New Year dawns, when debts as well as clothing and food must be new. He will not stop until he finds me, and then—"

Frantic with worry, Fu Be Be interrupted relentlessly, "That is your affair. You bought the watch—now it is for you to manage your creditor."

Miserably Young Fu went about the following day's tasks. In the afternoon, having found no possible solution to his problem of settling the debt, he decided that he might at least escape from Chungking and Old Hsui's search until the New Year had passed. Tang, with true holiday spirit, gave all permission to leave early, and Young Fu wasted no time in putting his own plan into action.

On several occasions his mother had mentioned a nephew, the son of her oldest brother, who was said to live in the hills across the Yangtze. Her brother was no longer on this earth, but his wife, she believed, still lived. Some day she hoped to go see for herself. It would be good to walk in the country once more and better still to renew bonds with members of her family. And now it was he, not his mother, Young Fu told himself with a rueful smile, who would first meet these cousins—and under what humiliating circumstances!

At the river's edge he asked a boatman for the privilege of helping to load vegetables and thereby earned a free ride across to the other bank. There he nodded his thanks, then walked slowly up the path to the first village on the hill. His blue cotton jacket and trousers flapped in the sharp wind, and misty fragments of the leaden sky stretched out damp, cold fingers and clung to him, satisfied with having found a permanent resting place. He shivered. Colder off here in the hills, and in the little moneybag tied within his belt, just eight coppers! And here he was, on the eve of the most important holiday of the year, a fugitive from home and Chungking. And all because he had been unable to resist Hsui's flattery! Miserably he shrugged the thought away, and, entering the village, slipped into the tea house and ordered a bowl of steaming tea.

The road winding past was busy with traffic. Ornate sedan chairs, hung with heavy satin and gay tassels, pushed by on the shoulders of chair-bearers in livery. Here and there a small, open, reed basket held a traveler who had made the arduous trip over the mountains, and threading in and out were hired street chairs, cracked and scarred, looking as if they might drop their occupants along the roadside any minute.

Young Fu watched the unceasing stream make its bustling way down to the river bank, there to be ferried across the Yangtze to Chungking. Exiles they were, living in other sections for various reasons, and now returning with their families for the New Year's festivities to Chungking, where they had been born. No man in all China but would make the journey home at this season, regardless of weather or any other circumstance that might be against him. The one essential was money and a clear record. And that, Young Fu reminded himself dismally, was just what he did not, at the moment, possess. Otherwise he would now be with his mother in their room in Old Dai's tenement.

Poor as he knew it to be, longing added to distance made it seem more desirable than the halls in the Governor's *ya-men*. There would be charcoal in the brazier to warm his cold hands and feet and, as for food, Fu Be Be starved cheerfully enough the rest of the year, but there was no stinting about what she considered suitable for offering the gods. And when the gods had partaken of all they wished, that which remained was shared by the household. Young Fu's mouth watered as he thought of delectable dishes, rich in Szechuen spices and swimming in incomparable sauces.

Also, in the weeks past, his mother had made for each of them a new outfit of clothing and a pair of black sateen shoes, sewed with thousands of delicate stitches. The shoe soles, made of scraps of paper and cardboard found on the streets and pasted together, she had covered with stout cloth, and then with her needle had traced a design of symmetry and beauty.

One night coming down late from Wang Scholar's room, her son had been touched by the bent, weary figure devoting itself with such painstaking effort to the pattern of the sole. "Why do you spend your heart?" he asked. "One wearing on these slimy pavings will ruin them. Look at my sandals bought five days since! Already much of the straw is cut through."

That there was truth in what he said, Fu Be Be knew. Never had she imagined streets so filthy as those in Chungking. The footways and flights of steps were wet and slippery always with the drippings of the city's water supply, for Chungking utilized her rivers in more ways than one. Daily, uncounted coolies passed through the water gates, filled the buckets suspended from their carrying poles, and retraced their steps slowly and painfully back to the city heights. Daily was this done many times, that the hundreds of thousands within her walls might drink and be cleansed.

"Why waste material and strength, if not to make good shoes?" she countered, squinting eyes that were half-blind from loss of sleep.

But thinking over lost delights of food and clothing would not gain him a night's shelter now, Young Fu said to himself. He paid for the tea and inquired the location of the cousin's farm. The name was recognized and directions given. As he climbed the winding paths between the terraced fields, the cold became more intense and it was a relief to find himself at last descending into the little valley where the farm lay.

The house, solidly black against the night's shadows, was folded in quietness. Young Fu rapped sharply and someone called out, "Who is there?"

"It is Fu Yuin-fah, the son of your father's younger sister, and I have just come from Chungking."

"What proof have I that you are that one?"

Young Fu recalled scraps of family history, gleaned from Fu Be Be's conversations, and repeated them. After a drawing of bolts, the door was opened a crack, and a small paper lantern flickered over the outsider. Satisfied about the harmlessness of this slender boy, the farmer invited him in, asking as he secured the door, "Why are you here at this hour?"

Young Fu explained over the tea and sweetened eggs, hastily prepared for him by his cousin's wife. The family stood about him shivering sleepily while he confessed that he owed a debt and was hiding overnight from his creditor. There was much shaking of heads over such an affair, and the farmer counseled against the evil of buying that which one could not afford. In a corner the grandmother, wrapped snugly in her *pu-gai*, mumbled her sympathy for the poor mother on whom he had brought disgrace. Young Fu became more wretched with each remark and thought that even the cold winds and the hills might be preferable to this chiding. But it soon ceased. He was given a comfortable place to sleep and the house settled into silence once more.

It was still dark next morning when the others began to move about. The visitor stretched, then was startled from his drowsiness by a hubbub at the door.

"*Kuai lai* (Come quickly)!" called the farmer.

Young Fu unrolled his comfort and went to join the others. Outside there was a strange whiteness in the air and small pieces of soft down fluttered about their heads and settled on their garments.

"Feathers!" exclaimed the youth.

"No, snow!" contradicted his host.

Young Fu and the children of the household looked about them in amazement. "So this is truly snow, is it?" he asked the farmer again. "I have never seen any before."

"I, myself, have seen it only twice—once when I was a boy and again this morning. It is very strange."

They entered the house again. Young Fu had caught up a handful of powdery flakes from the ground, and now he showed them to the wife and grandmother. The old woman rested her two, tiny, bound feet on a hot brazier and puffed at a water pipe. She touched a finger to the snow in his hand.

"In my youth," she said, "they would have called this a good omen for the New Year, it is the wintry breath of the Dragon."

"Ai-ya!" exclaimed Young Fu, "it is gone!" He looked with dismay at his wet hand.

The old grandmother chuckled. "With the coming of spring heat, winter dies; so with this. Your hand was warm."

Young Fu walked to the door, and stepping outside again looked at the country about him, mistily outlined in the dawn. Hills, fields, trees, even the twisting paths lay bewitched under the spell of this white magic. Beautiful like white jade, he thought; soft, like silk in a cocoon. "Dragon's Breath!" He gazed about him with renewed interest. "Dragon's Breath!" he repeated.

Reentering the house, he asked the farmer, "Have you two large *mei-shiang-tz* to lend me?"

"Perhaps," was the reply. "For what use?"

"I wish to fill them with snow to take to Chungking."

"Why trouble to carry snow all of the way to Chungking?"

"*Lao Po Po* (Grandmother) calls it the breath of the Dragon, and says it brings good fortune; once there I shall sell it to pay my debt," answered Young Fu.

The grandmother removed the pipe from her mouth. "It is not wise to do this. You may offend the Dragon, and then—" she stopped abruptly. She had been ready to predict misfortune, and no one knew better than she the danger of mentioning such things as poverty and illness and trouble on New Year's Day. That was the surest way to bring them down upon one's head for the whole year. Let this foolish youth go about his business; she would have nothing more to say. She took up her pipe again.

After a heaping bowl of food and another of hot

water, the baskets were forthcoming. Young Fu thanked them gratefully and, wishing them the finest prosperity the New Year might bring, he started out.

Daylight was not yet full, and the snow continued to lend its glamour to the world. He turned and called back a final *"Gong Hsi Go Nien* (New Year Greetings) !" which echoed through the hills about him.

Hurrying on his way, he halted only when he noticed that the snow was becoming less thickly spread. Here he filled his baskets, packing the cold, white substance into a compact mass. He did not stop again until the bank of the river had been reached. It was just as he had hoped—down here there was no sign of the snowfall, and certainly there would be none in the city. He glanced along the shore for a boat. His fear had been that he might have to wait too long; there was not likely to be much traffic on the river today, for no one, unless he were forced to it, would work—boatmen included. A hundred yards to the left a boat seemed to be pushing off. Young Fu ran, yelling as he did so.

The boatman looked up from his load of oranges. "Ten coppers for a ride today," he called out.

"I can give you something better than coppers," gasped the youth, and swung himself aboard.

Breathing more easily after a moment or two, he reached within a basket and shaped a lump of its contents into a ball. This he held before the man's astonished eyes.

"What is it?" came the question.

82 |

"Dragon's Breath from the hills," replied Young Fu. "It means fortune for the New Year."

"So!" remarked the boatman, very much impressed, and laid it on the floor close to where he stood.

In a short time they reached the Chungking side of the river. Young Fu lifted his carrying pole and climbed the steep steps to a city gate. Once within, he swung ahead to a busy thoroughfare, far from the haunts of Hsui, or those of his own friends. He located a niche in a corner of a stone wall and settled himself for business. His lips puffed out a long breath of relief. At least he was safe in his own city once more and, if all went well, he would soon be at home. He began to call his strange merchandise for sale.

Nine o'clock had come, and Chungking had risen early in honor of the New Year. Within the homes there had been the ceremony of the kitchen god's return, followed by an elaborate breakfast. Now, robed in new finery, her people were about to start the day's round of excitement. Gaiety was in the air. Bunting, multicolored, floated in the narrow streets above the people's heads; from dingy house fronts fluttered handsome banners, bright with gold characters, expressing the season's best wishes. Lacepaper ornaments, and pictures of Kwan-Yin, Goddess of Mercy, Kwan-Tih, God of Protection, and other important members of the heavenly circle shared places of honor. Fantastic lanterns and toys of every description were being offered for sale. New Year was here and all China was preparing to enjoy it.

"Dragon's Breath from the hills" . . .

Crowds, chattering noisily, began to fill the streets. Young Fu, crying his ware with the full strength of his lungs, soon attracted their attention. Immediately the throng pressed about him.

"What is it? What is its use?" they asked.

"It is Winter Dragon's Breath come down from the hills. Hold but a little in your hand and good fortune will follow through the year! Five coppers for a touch of it—only five coppers for 'fortune's smile!' "

Fingers reached out. "Give it to the little *Hsien-Seng!* Here, Small Tamer of Tigers, take it in thy hand! It burns thee? Yes, but for a moment; it is the breath of the Dragon."

"Wee Sister, do not fear! It is good for thee to have; it will shield thee from harm."

Trade was thriving, and Young Fu's hands ached with cold. Coppers had been pouring into the little moneybag, and he welcomed a moment of respite as the laughing people moved away. He folded his hands within opposite sleeves in an endeavor to warm them before he called to another group which was approaching. For an hour he stood there, alternately selling snow and thawing his frozen fingers, and at last there was nothing left in each *mei-shiang-tz* but tiny pools of water.

Young Fu shouldered his empty baskets and walked toward his own section of the city. A li from Hsui's shop, he sat down on a doorstep and lifted the coin bag from his belt. He counted carefully—three dollars, and forty coppers over! Back into the bag he thrust the change, and made directly for Hsui's establishment.

The store was boarded up for the holiday, but a series of knocks soon brought the proprietor himself to the entrance. In his hand he swung a lighted lantern. Sliding back the panel to its full width, he stared at Young Fu in amazement. "What do you want and where have you been hiding?"

The boy grimaced at the sight of the lantern. Hsui, along with other business men, would through the hours of today's sunlight carry a lantern, thereby announcing to his debtors that for them the New Year had not yet dawned. The name Fu, at least, was no longer among these unfortunates. Suddenly he looked Hsui full in the face. "I wish to pay my debt; as for where I have been, that is my affair." He pushed the money toward the other. "Give me the little paper now!" he demanded.

The transaction completed to his satisfaction, he stepped into the street again. For the first time in weeks, he breathed freely. His account with Hsui was closed, he was back in Chungking with the day still young, and in his moneybag were forty coppers. Truly, the breath of the Dragon had meant good fortune to him.

"Open the door!" he shouted when he arrived at Dai's.

Fu Be Be lifted the latch, then watched him enter with fear in her eyes. "Did he find you?" she asked.

"That is an affair of the past," replied her son. "I was able to discover a way out and the matter is settled."

"When did you acquire so much ability, Honorable One?"

Young Fu smiled knowingly, then explained. His

mother was speechless. Reaching into his belt, he drew out the forty coppers. "Here is a New Year's present toward your coffin," he said, and placed them in her palms. Her eyes softened.

"Tell me," he insisted as he stretched across the table for some fruit, "am I still the most stupid member our family has produced?"

Fu Be Be did not reply. There was no need to remind him that two good dollars of her money had gone into the debt. That he had earned this astonishing amount today, and in so unheard of a fashion, was proof enough that his head was not empty. She hid the coins under a loose brick in the chimney and smiled to herself. The spirits of their ancestors hovering at this season over the rooftree need not now be ashamed of their young representative's actions. A sigh of relief passed between her lips. Fortune augured well for the coming year!

At Tang's, the holiday ended, Young Fu did not boast of his adventure, although the temptation to do so was strong. Only the latter half of the affair was to his credit, and if he told that, the first would naturally leak out. Once or twice he was on the point of confiding in Small Li, but he held his tongue. It was just as well that no one else knew how much of a fool he had had to be in order to prove his cleverness. Hsui and the matter of the foreign watch would have to sink into the silent depths of memory and there remain.

TILTING
WITH
FIRE

THREE MONTHS LATER, on his way to deliver ten small kettles to the new tea house, Young Fu glanced at Old Hsui's jewel shop and sniffed. Only a little more than three moons had passed since he had not dared to enter this roadway; he drew a long breath as he remembered how it had tested his wits to avoid Hsui in other sections of the city. But now, his debt in the past, he found pleasure in showing his former creditor how little he thought of the stock on display. Almost daily he sought the excuse of some errand for passing this way; as often, Old Hsui, fully aware of his presence, failed to see him. That Hsui was annoyed, his tormentor had no doubt. In selling him the worthless foreign watch, the jeweler had cheated him of five dollars, and by this method Young Fu felt he was getting his money's value, cash by cash.

A sudden stirring in the bedlam of the street drew his attention from the shop. Segments of traffic—load-coolies, sedan chairs, pedestrians—flew back like clods under a keen-edged plow as an advance guard of soldiers cleared a furrow for an official chair, held high on the shoulders of uniformed coolies. Young Fu pressed close to a wall. He did not breathe freely until the rear guard had passed from sight. To a youth of his age, soldiers on the Chungking streets offered a constant menace. Only too many, as in his own miserable experience, had been seized for military service. Sometimes, most awful fate of all, they were sent down the river as trackers, to pull boats over the swirling waters of the great gorges. Those who returned came back broken in body and spirit.

Wang Scholar said that most of men's troubles came from war. For centuries the Classics had taught the foolishness of fighting; but men refused to heed wisdom, and suffered accordingly. As a result, Chungking in its important position was a shuttlecock kicked about among the opposing forces, and held for the moment by that general who had the most strength in his toe. Issues were so confused that it was difficult for the man in the street to follow events, and unless one had a shop to be looted, or youth with which to fight, it made little difference. Life went on as usual; tea houses were opened and copper kettles made, much as if the province were at peace.

Arriving at the tea house, Young Fu found the place crowded with customers, and the proprietor, elated by so auspicious a beginning, signed for the kettles and offered the apprentice a bowl of tea. The youth accepted it gravely. Here was someone who treated him with respect. Reluctantly he left the gaiety of the place and sauntered back to Tang's.

The air was heavy with steaming sunshine, and cracks between the flagstones of the street hissed through the accumulated filth of ages, like miniature geysers; beggars searched for unwelcome life within their tatters; indescribable odors of refuse and decay assailed the nostrils. But for a season rain was gone, and across the river the hills, for the second time in his life in Chungking, changed garments of azalea for orchid and wild rose. Every shop boasted a spray of bloom. Young Fu halted by one counter's vase of shrub and breathed deeply. Something sharp rose above the flower's perfume. It was smoke. The sky revealed no signs of fire. Probably some woman had dropped a rag on her charcoal cook pan.

When he reached the coppersmith's, they were eating midday food. Young Fu reached for his bowl, but ate little. The tea he had drunk spoiled his taste for this. Later he and Small Li stretched in a sunny corner, cracked a half-dozen watermelon seeds acquired at the tea house, and extracted the appetizing kernels. Tang and the older men smoked. From a distance came the sound of shots. It caused no excitement; shots were as familiar to Chungking ears as the cawing of magpies. The youth recalled the official chair. He mentioned it.

"Whose was it?" questioned Tang, with some show of interest.

"I did not hear."

The coppersmith removed his pipe. "Probably Hsu's or some lesser officer's. The gods be thanked that Hsu is once more in power and that rotten egg, Liu, defeated!"

"What did Hsu do to him?"

"Nothing—great is our misfortune!" Tang sighed. "He escaped with most of his officers, but that he has left the city is unlikely. His chief supporters are here, and Hsu will carry his heart in his hand until the other lies dead before him, for Liu, devil that he is, will stop at nothing to further his affairs."

They returned to work. During the afternoon Small Li, back from an errand, called out that fire burned without the city wall, just below the foreign hospital. Young Fu did not move his gaze from his soldering. That might have been what he smelled on the street at noon. Well, if it were in that quarter, he did not have to fear for his mother's room on Chair-Makers' Way.

At dusk he hurried home. The air was acrid. Charred bits hovered uncertainly above, until shifting currents surprised them into forced landings on roof or paving. People accosted one another for information. Young Fu entered his own door and sat down to the bowl of food that his mother shared with him. Lowering her voice, she asked about the fire. He replied that he knew little, but as soon as he finished this *mein*, which was certainly of a better flavor than that he had just eaten at Tang's, he would go see for himself.

Fu Be Be's jaw sagged with terror. "Do you wish us to burn, also?" she demanded. "From your birth I have taught you that when the Fire Dragon chooses a victim, there is only one thing to do, and that is to keep out of sight. To interfere is to bring disaster on your own roof."

Young Fu stuffed the remaining *mein* into his mouth and rose. "If the Dragon wishes to devour the foreigner's hospital, it is not my business. I go merely to watch."

Fu Be Be scolded her dismay. "That is the trouble with youth—always prying into what is not its affair. When I was your age, I listened to my elders, but now! It is not necessary to interfere actively with the Dragon; an expression of pity for an unfortunate victim may attract its enmity. Safety lies in distance from the scene of calamity."

Her son smiled at her fears. "I will hide in the crowd," he promised, "and the Dragon will not know of my presence." Before she could check him, he had slipped through the doorway and was gone.

Fu Be Be stood still, a gloomy figure of impending trouble. Would her son never learn wisdom? From her small store of money she took three cash. Closing the door firmly behind her, she went out to the street. She moved as swiftly as her tiny, bound feet would carry her toward the Goddess of Mercy's shrine. Three cash were three cash but, invested in incense immediately, they might ward off the danger that he was so openly courting.

The offering attended to, she went slowly home. It was too dark to sew. For a time she leaned in her doorway and listened to the talk of neighbors. The sky above her reddened. Trembling she sought her room.

Young Fu, nearing the foreign property, stopped to wipe smarting eyes. Smoke pressed down into the narrow, winding streets, and made breathing difficult. He was within a few feet of the compound gate. For a minute he dallied with fear of the Fire Demon. Suppose his mother were right! Then curiosity won. He slipped between the great wooden doors.

Never had he seen anything like it. The broad expanse of yard and garden was filled with refugees from the huts below the city wall. Their cries were deafening. Mothers ran about screaming for strayed children. Two men fought for possession of a pigskin trunk. An old man held a tray of peanuts, his entire stock, close to his breast; in the jostling crowd they rolled away from him to be crushed underfoot. Beneath a palm a woman, her white hair scorched brown, wailed for her husband. Patients from the hospital lay helpless on stretchers placed against the wall. But the fire was magnificent. The foreign hospital, so much higher than most Chinese buildings, leaped to three times its size in flame and smoke. As yet the school and the house were untouched, and so long as the wind continued toward the river, they were likely to remain so.

He pushed between the distraught people for a better view. Chinese women, in strange blue-and-white uniforms, carried in more patients. Their faces were black with soot; their clothes torn and discolored. A foreign woman with yellow hair was there. She gave orders rapidly.

Young Fu watched her curiously. He had seen any number of foreigners in these two years, of course, but he had not been so close to one of their women before. What astonished him was that a woman should be in authority at a time like this. He heard her tell the uniformed nurses to take the patients to another hospital across the city. He wondered how they would do this. No chair-coolie would carry to safety one who had been rescued from the Fire Dragon's wrath. His eyes widened as he watched the Chinese women pick up the stretchers and start off with them. The next order was given to an elderly Chinese, evidently a head servant. He was to clear the grounds of refugees; it was no longer safe for them here; they would have to go out into the city.

Young Fu listened and slipped behind some shrubbery. The yellow-haired foreigner disappeared in the direction of the burning building. For more than an hour the stream of terrified and physically helpless flowed into the public highway. The compound slowly cleared. Then his eyes began to smart again. Smoke enveloped him.

Above the roar of the flames he heard a shriek, "The house! The house burns!" A fresh current of air cut through to him. There in the clearing atmosphere he saw the foreign woman. She was looking at the house. On the roof lay a burning ember, slowly eating its way between the water-soaked tiles. Cupping her hands about her mouth, she shouted, "Who will climb to the roof and knock off that piece of wood? All of our helpers are working in the burning hospital."

No one moved. Again she begged for a man's help, but the remaining onlookers were sidling toward the gateway. They knew what such an act might cost. One did not trifle with the spirits controlling the elements. Small flickers of light darted from the smoldering stick. She glanced about her pleadingly. Then she rushed into the house.

With interest, Young Fu watched her come out upon the second-story porch. She stepped on the railing and grasped an upright to the roof. He drew in his breath— the foreign woman herself would climb to the roof! The fact that a woman, even though foreign, would attempt that which men were afraid to do called forth admiration. Fascinated, his eyes clung to her; then he grinned. She had a brave heart, but of all the stupid ways to climb! That was no way to get a footing. Someone ought to tell her how. He stepped from his hiding place. Before he realized it, he had entered the house and was on the second-story porch, shouting to the foreigner, "Come down! Come down! I will show you the way to reach it."

Trembling, the woman slid to safety. He scrambled past her and up the column. A few paces along the edge and he was within arm's length of the burning wood.

Grasping a piece of broken tile, he stretched over . . .

Grasping a piece of broken tile, he stretched over, pushed at the firebrand, and watched it go hurtling to the yard below. Then scraping about with the tile, he crushed out the remaining sparks.

From where he knelt, he could see the raging caldron of destruction, which until this morning had been a refuge for the weary and ill, spit its contents of venom in all directions. Behind it lay the broken city wall and, spreading five hundred feet to the river below, a charred hillside was strewn with the wreckage of uncounted roof-trees. Truly the Fire Dragon had power! Suddenly the boy shivered: what was he doing here on this roof? With care he made his way down.

The foreign woman was waiting for him. "What is your name?" she asked. "And where do you live?"

Embarrassment seized the youth. This was the only time he had talked with a foreigner, except for that one brief contact with Tang's customer. Timidly he looked at her. She was leaning against the railing for support; her hair and eyebrows were singed; one hand was unnaturally red; holes were burned in a sleeve of her garment; her body shook with exhaustion. Understanding came to him. Here was nothing to fear. He answered her questions.

"You have saved the house," she continued. "Tomorrow I will send you a small gift of money—I have none tonight."

Something, much to his surprise, prompted him to say, "I wish no money."

"You have done us a great service and I will not forget. You were the only man here who was not afraid of the Fire Dragon."

Young Fu warmed to this speech. She had called him a man. "You, also, did not fear," he replied.

She managed a smile. "Not the Fire Dragon, of course, but of the climbing I was scared to death." She turned, and he silently followed her from the building.

Menservants were now carrying heavy boxes and piles of bedding into the yard. The foreigner called to them, "Did you save the office papers?"

"Most of them."

"One of you must watch the house roof."

Young Fu moved slowly to the gate. Halfway home he remembered that he would have to face his mother in a few minutes, and she would be stricken with terror. But the Fire Demon had not touched him, and the foreign woman had smiled at its power. Still, one could not say when it might take its revenge. Suppose that even now his mother was in danger. He ran toward Chair-Makers' Way.

There he found no sign of fire—only a thin veil of smoke which distributed itself impartially about the city. Fu Be Be was sitting in their room, waiting. "Where have you been so long?" she asked anxiously.

He lighted a candle before he spoke. He would tell his mother the whole story, otherwise she might imagine even worse things. When he had finished, she shook her head in despair, "You have brought ruin upon us."

"But nothing has happened."

"Tomorrow is still to come."

Neither slept. In the morning at Tang's, Small Den called out, "Did I not see you at the fire last night?"

Young Fu nodded.

The other went on, "Someone told me that later you helped the foreign woman. If you did, you were crazy! Misfortune will certainly find you."

Tang interrupted: "Lay down your hearts. What truth there is in this belief, I do not know, but twice in my life have I known men to interfere with the spirits—once to save a burning child, and once a man from the river— and punishment did not fall upon them. Also, while I care nothing for the foreigners, since most of their trade goes to my competitor, Wu, who should have been a water-coolie rather than a coppersmith, it was not the Fire Dragon who burned their hospital. Early yesterday morning, Liu's escaping troops, at his order, set fire to the houses without the wall. I told you he would stop at nothing."

Young Fu breathed more freely. Here was one of his own race who doubted. "The foreigners are not so different from us," he suggested.

Dsen, the journeyman, laughed. "How many moons have faded since you could not bear to look at one?" he inquired.

"That was when I was still very young."

Tang scowled at a flaw. "Having had but little experience with them, Source of Wisdom, I cannot say. I hope you will agree, though, that our faces show no resemblance!"

His apprentice grinned. He admitted readily that the foreigners were far from handsome.

At night his mother gave him a heavy envelope. A servant from the foreign school had left it for him just as she reached home. Young Fu opened it, grasped the enclosed packet in his fist, and studied the note. "I will ask Wang Scholar to help me," he said, and climbed the ladder to the teacher's room.

He returned immediately. With dignity he announced, "The foreign woman wished to thank me for saving her house; she enclosed a gift of five dollars."

"Five dollars!" gasped Fu Be Be.

"Five dollars. And today Tang himself said that he did not believe ten-tenths in the Dragon's power."

Fu Be Be sank to a seat. Her world was turning upside down. Five dollars! Truly the foreigners were mad creatures. It was more than she could earn in two months of labor. She stretched out a hand for the money.

But her son held it. "One half of one dollar of this I wish to use."

"I am not a foreigner to throw money away," she said sharply. "When you are a man, you may do as you please."

"Could a man have settled Hsui's debt better than I? One half of a dollar I must have."

"For what purpose?"

"I wish to buy a small kettle from Tang to give to the foreign woman."

His mother narrowed her eyes. Then slowly she agreed. A small gift was proper. He was becoming too much for her to manage. Her son was a fool, but a very wise one! She took the heavy coins from him and placed them safely away. She was glad she had offered the three cash in incense to Kwan Yin the night before. It might be wise to do the same tonight.

Young Fu ate some food and threw himself upon the bed. He was tired, and there was much to think about. At New Year's he had called the snow "Dragon's Breath," and sold it despite the warning of the old grandmother in the hills. Last night he had cheated fire of a house. Twice he had dared the spirits; twice good fortune had come to him as a result. There was something strange about it. Wondering, he fell asleep.

In the morning he took advantage of a moment in which Tang seemed unoccupied to ask about the small kettle. The coppersmith listened thoughtfully, then walked over to a shelf and reached for one that Old Tsu had just finished. Young Fu watched in delight. This, with its four squared sides sloping from top to bottom in lines of beauty, was worth a great deal more than he could afford. He waited for Tang to open the conversation.

"Take this to your foreigner and show her what can be done by a good artisan."

"You are giving me this for one half of a dollar?"

"Yes; if she has eyes to see, I shall not be the loser."

The apprentice wrapped it carefully and laid it aside. That night he carried the kettle to the foreign house. Bedlam still reigned inside the gate. Patients were being accommodated to the cramped quarters of house and porches. Charred remnants of the fire lay everywhere, and, beyond, the blackened ruins of the hospital cast somber shadows.

After a little while the woman with yellow hair appeared. "You wish to see me?" she asked with a nervous glance toward the tasks demanding her attention.

Young Fu bowed. "I wish to thank you many times for the money you sent. What I did was not deserving of such an amount."

She smiled. "It was worth much more than that to me."

Another bow acknowledged this remark. "I wish to present to you this small and undesirable gift." He extended with two hands the kettle.

Murmuring her thanks, the foreigner accepted the article and removed the tissue covering. Her eyes opened widely. "I do not understand. This is a beautiful piece of brass, much too fine for me to take from you. Where did you get it?"

"At the shop where I am apprenticed. My master, the coppersmith, does only this kind of work—he is an artisan of rare ability."

"Why have I not heard of him? I did not know there was brass like this in Chungking."

"That is but a poor specimen. You should see some of his better pieces. He has the best reputation," he hesitated for the most forceful ending possible, "this side of Peking"

The foreigner lost her worried expression and laughed aloud. "Certainly he lacks nothing in you, his apprentice! Some day when I have leisure, I shall visit his shop. Where is it, and what is his name?"

Young Fu told her and strolled homeward. His idea of a little gift and Tang's of a choice one had both in their way been wise. If the foreign woman transferred her patronage to Tang's shop, he would be given the credit. Good! He began to hum the strain which issued from a tea house close by. He wished he knew how to play on a lute. Wait a little, wait a little—everything came in time!

THE
DEVILS
OF
DISEASE

WITH THE ARRIVAL OF SUMMER, life became more difficult. Under a pitiless sky Chungking simmered. Fu Be
Be was again without work, and she fretted over the ex-
penditure of every separate cash. At the shop the journeymen bent over hissing anvils, and Young Fu and
Small Li sweltered in the effort to keep the fire at proper

temperature. Errands offered no relief. The sun was as devouring as the flame that rose from the charcoal oven. Everyone was irritable. Men snarled at one another over trivial affairs that in cooler weather would have caused no comment whatever.

In the city there was talk of plague. The foreigners, it was said, would eat no meat at this season. Young Fu smiled to himself over such foolishness. As though animals had anything to do with cholera! It was sillier than Fu Be Be's belief that the Dragon controlled such affairs. Given the opportunity to eat good pork, he would prove how unimportant these ideas were. As for Dragons —he had less and less fear of them.

And then one morning Dsen, the journeyman, failed to appear. At noon, Tang with a grave face announced the workman's death. He had, it was claimed, eaten heartily at a feast given by a neighbor. The neighbor raised pigs and when they became unexpectedly ill he had killed them and preserved the meat. Most of it had been sold, but choice bits he had held for himself and intimate friends, among whom had been Dsen.

Silence fell over the group. Dsen had been popular. More than one would miss him.

Young Fu voiced the question, "Is it true that one can get cholera from eating bad meat?"

Murmurs of dissent arose. Tang spoke: "I am no doctor; I do not know. But that Dsen ate sick hog, and that he is no longer present, there is no doubt. This doctrine has come to the Middle Kingdom with the foreigners. And while they seem stupid in many ways, they have peculiar gifts in healing the body. In Peking, it is said, there is a large school in which our people study foreign methods of caring for the sick. But little faith have I in any doctor—it matters not which is his native land."

The tragedy of Dsen's death was forgotten in the scourge that settled its pall on Chungking. Cholera was followed by typhus, and Fu Be Be made daily offerings at Kwan Yin's little shrine. Babies were expected to die in the period of Great Heat, but this year every age contributed its share. Mothers and fathers, children and grandparents, slipped out of life with the passing of a day. The homes of the poor became less congested; the halls of the rich were filled with hired mourners; funeral processions crowded the streets; there were few doorways from which wailing did not issue.

The foreigners, all but those in charge of hospitals, had long since fled to the hills. Young Fu, sent on an errand to Tsu Chi Men, the gate through which one passed to take boat for the opposite shore, gazed longingly toward the slopes of green and wished for the weather he had seen there at New Year's. At the Spring Festival, Fu Be Be had crossed the river, and one of the cousin's children had met her at the water's edge and escorted her to the farm. She had returned from this excursion happier than at any time in Chungking. She had talked of nothing for days but the sweetness of the hill air, and the song a ricebird sang. Sometime she would go there again for a longer visit.

Her son, retracing his steps to the coppersmith's,

Funeral processions crowded the streets.

breathed in the strangling stench of drying hides that passed on loads bound for the tanneries, and remembered his mother's desire. That night he mentioned it.

"This, I think, would be a propitious time for you to go," he concluded.

"And leave you to the devils of disease?"

Young Fu smiled. "Wise men do not believe thus."

"And wise men die just as do fools. Hush!" she admonished severely when he would have spoken again, "are you mad that you offend the spirits with such talk?"

Her son said nothing further, and Fu Be Be stayed where she was.

It was much too hot to study in Wang Scholar's room. Instead, the old gentleman spent most of his leisure on the door sill. One evening he did not appear.

"Go to the honorable teacher's door and ask if he is well," Fu Be Be suggested. "His face for days has worn the shadow of illness. This weather is as hard on the very old as on babes."

Young Fu dragged himself wearily up the ladder. Wang Scholar lay on his wooden pallet. His eyes opened slowly as the boy squatted beside him and asked, "Are you ill, sir?"

"I have no pain, but I am very tired. I would sleep." His eyes closed again.

When Fu Be Be heard this report, she pursed her lips. "Let me think a little. My grandmother used a certain brewing of herbs for such weakness." She moved to the chimney and took a coin from the hidden store. "Go to the large drug shop and buy these. Listen carefully while I repeat the names and quantities."

At the pharmacy, Young Fu watched with interest as the wizened old merchant prepared the order. The shop was filled with interesting things. Jars of liquids in which lizards and snakes were preserved in lifelike attitudes demanded attention. From the ceiling, strings of dried beetles and spiders swayed with each current of air. On the shelves were many boxes. Some of the names the youth could read—ground tiger tooth, newts' eyes, snail shell. But most fascinating of all was a huge red centipede, alive and active, in a tiny bamboo cage. Young Fu shivered as the horrid yellow head reared itself in the constant effort to escape.

Fu Be Be rose as he turned the corner of the street; she held out a hand for the package. When the brew had cooled a little, Young Fu carried it upstairs, and, assuming the role of authority, forced every drop between Wang Scholar's unwilling lips. Then catching up a fan, he sat down on the floor beside the old teacher and prepared to spend the night.

At midnight Wang Scholar roused. "Why art thou here?" he asked.

"Because you needed me. How are you now?"

"Better than for days. Thou art good beyond thy years."

"It is nothing. Now, sleep again! I will rest here beside you, Honorable Teacher."

The sky was light when a continued rapping on the door awoke them. From without Fu Be Be's voice warned her son, "Hurry!"

Wang Scholar clicked his teeth in dismay. "Thy master will scold thee, and the fault is mine!"

Young Fu smiled. "Do not worry!" he comforted with an assurance he was far from feeling. "I will see you again tonight; until then you must rest."

Fu Be Be pushed a bowl through a crack of the door. "Ask the Respected Scholar if he will condescend to eat this food; it will give him back the strength he needs."

Wang Scholar called his thanks, and mother and son hastened downstairs. Young Fu waited for nothing further. Like a shot he was off for the coppersmith's.

At his approach, Tang looked up sourly. "Are you a priest that you have so much leisure?"

The apprentice bowed. "I am sorry. Last night the teacher who dwells above us was ill. I stayed with him, and this morning I awoke a little late."

A spark of interest crept into Tang's eye. "A teacher? Who are you to have a teacher for your intimate?" he asked bluntly.

"My first night in this city, he spoke kindly to me; later he invited me to do books with him—" his voice trailed away leaving the sentence unfinished. This was the first time he had mentioned studying to anyone at the shop.

"You mean that you have been studying characters with a scholar?"

"Each evening, a little."

The master caught up a sheet of newspaper. "Read this!"

Young Fu selected a small item of local news and read

haltingly through it. Twice he stumbled on words he did not recognize, and Tang, looking over the boy's shoulder, prompted him. Small Den, who had entered the room hastily, stood still, his mouth gaping.

When Young Fu had finished, the coppersmith spoke to the other boy, "What do you wish?"

"Wen, the Mandarin, waits in the store."

"Tell him I come at once."

Den disappeared, and Young Fu, conscious that his hands were still trembling as a result of this testing, lifted his gaze to Tang's.

"Who is this teacher and where do you find money to pay him?"

"His honorable name is Wang, and he asks no payment."

"No payment! Truly you are a favorite of Heaven, for he has taught you well. I will talk with you again about this matter."

Tang was pleased, the youth told himself, as he watched the master make his way to the store. Instead of a scolding for tardiness, he had been commended for his ability in reading. He was beginning to believe that what Tang had just remarked was true; he must, indeed, be a favorite of the gods.

At the noon meal, Small Den brought the affair to the attention of the others. "How is our learned student at this hour?" he asked, bowing before Young Fu.

The journeymen looked up questioningly and Small Den responded to this sign of interest with an elaborate dramatization of what he had witnessed. One or two of the men laughed, but Old Tsu interrupted the speaker, "Would that you had sense enough to do something besides chatter! The fool always expends effort to make his superior seem less than himself."

Young Fu plunged his chopsticks into a bowl of white vegetable (cabbage) and calmly transferred a succulent portion to his own mound of rice. What Wang Scholar had tried to teach him was true, "When in trouble, silence is the best refuge." He had not opened his lips and the situation was entirely to his satisfaction.

Small Li, sitting next him, leaned over to whisper, "That is why you ceased watching the public letter writer near the foreign temple, is it not so?"

His companion nodded.

"But you did not tell me the reason."

"I wished to do so. I—"

Li's face became downcast. "I understand. I would have forgotten and told these others, and you did not wish them to know."

Young Fu caught up a tender morsel and pushed it into Small Li's mouth. "Lay down your heart!" he comforted. "That is but a little fault, and Wang Scholar says even the greatest men have their weaknesses."

The next day it was a consolation to recall the warm bond that held him and Li together, as he watched the other boy in the act of stoking the fire, stagger and then fall beside the oven. Young Fu yelled for help and rushed to the prostrate figure. Above the sound of pounding anvils, Lu caught the cry of distress and ran to assist.

Together they lifted the limp body and carried it to the coolest spot in the place, a corner of the store.

For a brief time all work ceased. Lu sent Den to a nearby shop for hot tea and forced some of the stimulant through the gray lips. Young Fu, certain that his friend was dead, fanned frantically. If only Tang were present!

As if in answer to the thought, the master appeared in the doorway. He glanced at the stricken apprentice, then called for a basin of cool water and a soft cloth. With these he bathed Li's head and wrists. After what seemed an interminable period to those watching, Small Li's eyelids quivered and his muscles began to jerk. With the first sign of recognition, Lu ordered, "Drink!"

Li obeyed, and Lu coaxed until the bowl was empty. "Heat in the stomach is what he needs," he explained as he refilled the dish.

Small Li opened his eyes, then closed them. Two scalding tears crept down his cheeks. "I want my mother!" he quavered.

Tang smiled understandingly. "When you are stronger, a sedan chair shall carry you to her," he promised.

"May I go with him?" Young Fu asked.

"Why you and not some other?"

"We are friends." His voice broke nervously. "I thought he was dead."

"Do not fear! Youth does not ascend the Dragon so easily, though this weather is sufficient to kill anyone."

The men returned to their work, and later Tang saw the two boys safely on the way to Li's home. The chair-bearers halted before the house on Chicken Street and a woman emerged. When she saw Li, she screamed, "What is the matter?"

Small Li attempted to answer, but his companion took the situation gravely in hand. "Your son became ill from too much leaning over the fire. He is better now. He wished to see you, his mother, and the coppersmith called a chair and sent him. He asked me to tell you that if tomorrow your son is not recovered, you may keep him with you for another day. Also, he says too much food is not good for this trouble; use soup or hot tea only, and let him sleep."

Li's mother, helping to carry the sick boy into the house, snapped her eyes angrily: "Eight children have I borne. Does your coppersmith think I know nothing, that he tells me how to care for this one? As for you, who have only lately been weaned from infancy, has your mother never taught you not to give advice to your elders?"

Young Fu held his tongue. What a temper she had; it was worse than Fu Be Be's! Small Li raised a hand in protest. "Please, Good Mother, please do not scold Fu! He is my best friend." He turned wearily to the wall at the side of his bed, and the other apprentice gave a last grip to the fevered hand, and slipped into the street.

That Li had not sufficient strength to return on the morrow was evident, for the following day failed, also, to mark his appearance. Young Fu, paying calls at the house on Chicken Street each night after work, brought the news to Tang. Li, with his right leg drawn up in agonizing pain, lay almost motionless, but his moans resembled those of one possessed with evil spirits.

His mother, recognizing the friendship between the two boys, now confided her worry to the other apprentice. "The gods are offended. I have been careless about paying them any attention, and in revenge they will take my firstborn from me. It is possible that if we call in the priests, he may yet be saved, but my husband will not agree. He thinks the priests have little power; they demand much money for coming, and do nothing to earn it. But they have strange ways, which we do not understand, of exorcising evil spirits and if they can cure my son, I will help to earn the money to pay them."

Tang listened to this report and drew his brows together in a frown. At midday rice he discussed the matter with the workmen. That he himself was in a quandary, he confessed. Lu interrupted with an instance of a friend who, supposed to be dying, had under the ministrations of priests recovered.

Old Tsu curled his lip grimly. "Yes, and my brother-in-law into whom priests plunged red-hot needles died."

Tang nodded. "More die than live. It is easy to leave this world after enduring their tortures. Li is a good youth. I wish that he might escape their clutches, but if his mother believes in them, I see no way out. The women always rule in such matters."

"Why not a doctor?" suggested the accountant.

"There is little difference in their methods."

"When my eldest grandson," Old Tsu broke in, "be-came sore of eye, his grandmother wished to place on them a poultice of herbs. In this way she had helped many with the same affliction. But the boy's mother, the most stupid woman under my roof, declared herbs were old-fashioned and demanded a doctor. At last, in order to quiet her tongue, my son, her husband, asked permis-sion to grant her request. Fool that I was, I gave it. The doctor came. Since that day my grandson moves like an old man. His eyes are darkened forever." A long sigh issued from the speaker.

Later in the afternoon, Young Fu walked up to the coppersmith. "The other day," he began hesitantly, "you said that the foreigners were reported to have a gift for healing. Do you think they might know how to help Li's trouble?"

"You are not too stupid! I myself had thought of them, but I still am not sure. Moreover, there is the problem of Li's parents. His mother is not likely to trust him to foreigners."

"On the other side, his father does not believe in the priests, nor does he wish to spend money on them. It might be my friend, the woman at the foreign hospital, could tell us."

Tang smiled. " 'My friend, the woman at the foreign hospital,' " he mocked, " 'my friend, the teacher'—and are there still others of whom I do not know?"

"Small Li," the boy's eyes lit daringly; he bowed low, "and unless I make a mistake—you, Honorable Copper-smith!"

"Ai-ya! but you give me credit for poor judgment."
Tang reached for a pipe and struggled to hide his amusement. "Enough of this nonsense for the present. Run to
the foreign hospital and learn what they can do to help
us!"

He pulled at his pipe until the boy was out of sight,
then chuckled to himself. This one was something new
in the way of an apprentice, and there was truth in what
he had just said. Some quality in the youth appealed to
him. His own son had died with the mother from smallpox years before, and there were moments when Tang
fancied a likeness between Young Fu and what his son
might have become. This youth had ambition and few
fears—and something more. His friends—Wang Scholar,
the foreign woman, himself—were proof enough of this
fact. As to the sort of man he would be, time alone could
prophesy.

An hour passed before Young Fu reappeared. "The
foreign woman was busy. I had to wait. When she came,
I told her about Li. She thinks it may be a very bad
disease which lasts for more than a moon. Should it be
that, then Li will surely die, she says; that is, if we leave
him to the priests and his mother. Even in the foreign
hospital, and the foreigners think they know more about
this illness than do we of the Middle Kingdom, people
die of it. It comes from drinking water that has not been
boiled." He scratched his head. "Ai, but they have
queer doctrines! Dsen dies of eating, and Li is ill from
drinking!"

"Did you learn nothing more than that the foreigners

have ways different from ours? Such information will be of no benefit to Li."

"No, this is but the beginning. I told her Li was my close friend and begged her to go look at him. At first she refused; his family had not invited her to do so and such a visit would not be according to custom. But after a little talk she consented. Tonight, with the foreign doctor, she goes to Li's home. If it should be the disease she mentioned, she will, with the consent of Li's parents, find a place for him in the foreign house which since the fire has been used as hospital. There they will do all that they know toward his recovery."

"Not so fast! Not so fast! Who can say whether Li's parents will agree?" interrupted Tang.

"That I do not know. However, it is true that a little word from the master in charge of an apprentice—" he let the sentence complete itself in thought.

"Fountain of Wisdom that you are! So I am to bear the responsibility! And suppose the foreigners kill him? For the rest of my life I suffer the demands of his family on my time and fortune."

"But if the foreigners can cure him, and left at home, he dies?"

"What do the foreigners ask for this service?"

"When I spoke of that, the foreign woman smiled. She said the price would be suited to what Li's father could afford to pay—a small amount, since he was, as I told her, a poor man with many mouths to feed."

"And they consider Small Li in spite of this. They must wish to fill empty beds."

"Their beds are filled, and the house, to overflowing. If Li goes to them, she does not yet know where they will place him."

Tang grunted. "Carry that jar to Wen Mandarin's residence and hurry! Den, who is tough, can take his turn at the fire."

That night Young Fu raced home through the heat. There he paused long enough to tell Fu Be Be that he would be later than usual and turned toward Chicken Street. He wished to prepare Small Li's mother for the unexpected visit of the foreigners, for Li Be Be was quite capable of chasing them from her threshold. She might, like many of the women, consider their coming a calamity and use any means to avoid contact with them.

When he arrived, Li's parents were quarreling violently; children crowded the room. Young Fu kicked a mangy dog through the doorway, and turned to the bed. At his friend's touch, the sick boy's hot hands reached for him and the parched lips muttered in pain. Li's fevered brain was restive under the turmoil of the room, and Young Fu, a lump welling in his throat, longed desperately to do something.

The parents paid no attention to the newcomer. The mother was screeching her determination to call in the priests; the father stood sullenly shaking his head in refusal. There was a rap at the doorway, and the younger children rushed to see. Young Fu looked up expectantly for the foreign women to appear; he was amazed to see the tall figure of Tang. In an instant the clamor lessened. A courteous exchange of greetings followed, the children were ordered to play without, and the older people settled in conversation. Only Small Li's whimperings never ceased. After a while, Tang rose and came to the bedside. He threw Young Fu a glance of understanding, then centered his interest on Li.

While he stood there, one of the children ran into the room. "Two foreign devils wait without," she announced in a scared voice.

"What do they wish?"

Young Fu jumped up. "One of them is my friend. She knows a great deal about sickness. I asked her to come to look at your son."

"Was that your business?" demanded Li's mother. "Never shall they see him!"

Her husband stepped forward, "I have as much faith in them as in the priests, and, as you well know, they cured the daughter of my youngest uncle." He moved to the door. "At least, it will do no harm for them to come in. Perhaps they know what this sickness is."

Li Be Be started to wail. As the women entered, Young Fu went to greet them. Tang bowed and stepped back into the shadow of the room. The foreigners addressed themselves to the father, "May we examine the boy?"

"Will you hurt him?"

The foreign doctor shook her head gravely, "No."

"Then do so; nothing can be worse than affairs at present."

Young Fu watched with interest. The doctor studied

her patient. "This is not typhoid, but something quite different. Usually it is not difficult to heal, but in your son the disease has gone so far, I cannot promise recovery. However, if you wish us to try, we shall carry him immediately to the foreign hospital and I shall attend to him at once."

"Why not here in his home?" Li's father wished to know.

"I have not the proper instruments and medicines to use. My only hope for him is to get to the foreign hospital as soon as we can. The decision rests with you."

Young Fu hung breathless on the reply. Li Be Be cried afresh, "They will kill my first born. They will kill him!"

The father was making up his mind with difficulty. "And the cost?"

"Whatever you can afford to pay."

"That is fair. And if he stays here, he is likely to die, and if the priests come, most surely. He may go with you."

Li Be Be darted forward. "Then I go with him."

The foreign doctor smiled in understanding. "Of course, and his father may come, too, to keep you company while we are operating."

Tang came from the shadows and spoke to the father. "If the boy needs anything for which you cannot pay, let me know." He beckoned to Young Fu and they went into the street together.

The next morning a younger brother bore word to the shop that Small Li was still alive. Four days later Young

Fu was permitted to see the patient for a few minutes. The sick boy smiled weakly. Heat had left his body and he was no longer in pain. It would be almost a moon, however, before he could leave the hospital—his attack of appendicitis had been a severe one.

Young Fu walked through the gateway thinking happily of the good fortune which had come from knowing the foreign woman. Her five dollars had added to his mother's slim resources; his small gift of a brass kettle had brought her trade to Tang; and now his friend's life had been saved. He wondered at his own luck. Evil spirits and foreigners were two things his mother's generation considered it wise to fear. He had, according to them, been dangerously unwise. And the result in each instance had been increased prosperity and happiness.

A funeral procession with elaborately robed priests beating gongs and chanting weird rhythms met him. He stepped to the curb and watched with interest the coolies, dressed in white mourning cloth, who carried aloft paper imitations of articles the dead might wish to use in the spirit world. Young Fu shivered. Sadness tinged his thoughts as he remembered that the genial Dsen would not again work at an anvil. But Wang Scholar and Small Li were both recovering rapidly. And in a few days the period of Great Heat would fade and White Dew's coolness would give men new vigor. No hardship lasted forever!

A FOOTSTOOL FOR BANDITS!

BEFORE FU REALIZED IT, White Dew had slipped into winter. Small Li was again at work, and a strange man, named Wei, sat at Dsen's anvil. With the newcomer came discord. Old Tsu, as chief designer, held undisputed sway, and Lu, in charge of welding, worked hand in glove with his small, elderly friend in assigning tasks to the other journeymen and apprentices. No artisan until Wei had ever questioned their authority in managing the workrooms. He it was who dared to suggest changes in Old Tsu's cunning designs, who informed Lu that the welding might be improved, who offered Tang none of the respect and courtesy due a proprietor from one of his employees.

As the days passed, Young Fu and the others in the establishment waited with interest for destruction to seek out the newcomer, but nothing happened. Old Tsu's expression, when it rested on Wei, changed from cynical amusement to active ill humor; Lu's sharp voice acquired a thinner edge in giving orders; Tang seemed entirely unaware of what was happening under his nose. But each hour the workshop felt more keenly the loss of the genial Dsen.

And then the subject of Wei was overshadowed by the greater one of politics. Chungking had experienced more fighting, and a new governor controlled Szechuen Province. How long he would remain in office was as much a matter of conjecture as the sort of executive he would make.

There was common talk of a government at Nanking. Peking, for the first time in centuries, did not bear its name "Northern Capital." It had become instead, "Peiping," Northern Peace. Names—Sun Yat-sen, Chiang Kai-shek, Feng Yu-hsiang—seeped through to Chungking's inattentive ears. One of these men was dead, and in Nanking, so it was reported, people were spending fabulous sums to build a monument to his memory.

This much Young Fu gleaned, though which man was dead he could not say. Nor did he know what deeds the monument was supposed to commemorate. The West was still only faintly touched by the enormous popularity of the dead Sun Yat-sen, whose patriotism and statesmanship while he was living had made him a symbol of New China's hope. What concerned the youth more vitally was the fact that Peking was no longer Peking.

When he spoke to Tang about it, the coppersmith opened his hands in a gesture that dismissed politics from the problems with which the average man had to deal. "The Nationalists, as these Southerners call themselves," he explained, "have chosen Nanking for their capital, I have heard, because it lies nearer the center of the kingdom. True it is, however, that Nanking will be easier for them to hold than Peking, which is not only far north, but remains in the hands of their enemies."

"Are these Nationalists great Tuchuns?"

"Tuchuns there are in plenty; no doubt, though, from what I have heard, the Nationalist Government promises to do something more than loot. Two days since, at a meeting of the guild, a man from Hankow spoke at length concerning the southern army's plans. They wish to copy many of the foreigner's ways of living—among them good roads, hospitals, and schools that even the poor may attend. These are all good, but for me the worth of some of their ideas has yet to be proved."

"And where will they spend this money—in the south?"

"Some of it here in Chungking. It is said they will

build a road to Dsen-Gia-Ngai which will branch out to Tzechow, Suining, and Chengtu."

"What is wrong with the stone roads already there?" Young Fu wished to know.

"Too narrow, they claim, for the large carts they will use in which twenty people can travel at once." Tang paused to laugh. "I asked whether donkeys or men would pull these carriages, and the man from Hankow replied, 'Neither, they will run by themselves.' I saw that was his way of joking and did not press the matter. What troubles me is the question of who will pay for all of these improvements. It may be they have some way of taking loot from their generals and using it for the good of the country, though that is even less likely to happen than carts to run without help. This new governor is said to be one of their men. We shall see if he is any different from a hundred others."

Indirectly, the new Tuchun affected Tang at an early date. From the officials of Hochow, a city on the Lin River, came an order for a gift of brasses to be presented to His Excellency. The coppersmith was elated over this large, out-of-town commission; it was another proof of his growing reputation for fine work. When it was finished, the whole shop breathed with relief. Tang had taken such pains to see that each item was executed perfectly that they were glad when the last shining piece was off their hands. At the last moment, the master decided to attend personally to the delivery. He turned to Young Fu.

"Since you seem to have no fear of devils, you may

go with me. River bandits are simply devils in another form, and it may be you will escape their attention as well as you did the Fire Dragon in the past. Either you have the special favor of Kwan Yin or you are of so little importance that even the devils pass you by!"

The apprentice grinned in reply. He was too happy for speech. For days he had been hoping that he might accompany whoever went on the trip to Hochow, but he had not dared to think about it too much. And now that it was Tang who was going, the favor was doubly to be desired.

Tang's attention was diverted and Small Li, with a sheet of metal in his hands, stopped to whisper, "Do you wish to go?"

His friend stared at him in surprise. "Naturally!"

"Why naturally? I, for one, do not. It is said the *ban-keh* are thick on both sides of the river. You will not reach the town of Tu-to."

Young Fu laughed. "Many things are said. 'The coward mistakes a rock for a tiger.' There is much travel on the Little River and the *ban-keh* cannot stop everyone. We have as good a chance as any. Moreover, the Hochow officials have sent down an escort of soldiers."

It was Small Li's turn. "When," he demanded, "were soldiers known to face bandits? They will desert you at the first sign of danger. No, I prefer to stay in Chungking and work at pots. I sleep better with the city gates barred between me and such visitors."

He moved hastily away as Tang came up and addressed Young Fu. "The day is almost ended," he said.

"Go to your home and prepare to meet me at dawn tomorrow morning, just within the Lin River Gate."

Young Fu hurried through the streets. Why Tang had chosen him he did not know, though it might in some way be connected with the foreign woman's patronage. True to her word, she had come and purchased, and later sent her cook back for more samples. In Chair-Makers' Way his steps slowed. His mother, he realized suddenly, was not likely to rejoice with him over this honor. If the river were safe, she would envy him this chance to return to their native district, but not now when the air was rife with bandit tales. Fu Be Be, he was thankful to remember, could not forbid his going. As an apprentice, he followed the rules of the establishment rather than those of the home.

When she returned at dusk from the bristle shop, she showed her surprise. "Have you sickness, or has your master tired of your incompetence?"

Her son's expression was mischievous. "Neither, Most Honorable Parent! Behold in me the one preferred above all others in the shop!"

Fu Be Be raised one hand as a shield to her eyes. "Your importance blinds me," she said with sarcasm. "Do not tell me that the new Tuchun has asked for your release from Tang, that you may help in governing the province."

Her son chuckled, then his face resumed its mock gravity. "No, but I go to serve him, nevertheless."

Fu Be Be's lower jaw sagged. "What?" she cried.

"Tomorrow at dawn, Tang leaves for Hochow to

deliver the brasses which are to be a gift to His Excellency from the Hochow officials—and I go with him."

She picked up her work again. "Of course, and after a good sleep the coppersmith will decide that you are a better representative than himself, and he will remain here to do your work in the shop." She was still jibing, but her words carried an undertone of anxiety.

Young Fu recognized this and changed to seriousness. "What I have said is true, Deeply Respected Mother; Tang told me today; that is why I am home early."

His mother's voice became shrill. "Is it your meaning that you go with them to Hochow?"

For answer, the boy nodded.

"Is Tang a newcomer to talk of travel on the Little River? Has he never heard of bandits? Only a mile above Chungking have they their first stronghold, it is said. There was T'sen, the mandarin, captured, his goods taken, and his body beaten so badly that he will not recover. Does Tang wish the same fate? And even if he does, why must he take you? Why not Li who has brothers? Does he not know that I have no one but you?" Tears began to creep down her cheeks.

Young Fu strove to comfort her. "Tang was not born yesterday; he knows that to send the brasses by someone else would be almost certain loss. Only too many messengers have used the excuse of bandits to steal goods for their own profit. Finer work has not been done in Chungking, and the master is unwilling to trust its delivery to hands other than his own. An escort of soldiers will go along."

129

Fu Be Be wailed: "Now you are certain to be ruined! Is it not a byword that to have soldiers is an added danger, since it is the easiest way for the *ban-keh* to acquire guns and ammunition? I myself will ask Tang to take another in your place."

Her son's heart sank. "Is Tang likely to be pleased with such a request?" he asked quietly. "Many youths in this city wait to fill my vacancy as his apprentice. There is no better coppersmith under whom to learn. This very order proves the truth of those words. After a few years I shall know enough to open my own place, and if I am known as Tang's apprentice, trade will come easily."

She screwed up her eyes. Open a shop—this was something new. "Where would you find money to start a business?"

He smiled. "That is not today's worry. Lay down your heart! When that time comes, you shall have a small slave girl to do your bidding, and jade ornaments shall gleam in your hair!"

Fu Be Be sighed. She might as well accept calmly what life brought of good or ill. "What will you need besides your bedding?" she asked.

"Only my long blue garment to wear over these. I wish to look like Tang's first assistant, not his coolie."

The morning dawned fresh and crisp under the biting breath of winter. For the first two hours of sailing Young Fu shivered behind his roll of bedding. The soldiers, ten in number, crowded one end of the boat. For the youth their presence added uneasiness. With a superior air they discussed previous dangerous exploits. Tang filled a brass water pipe and pulled at it. The oarsmen rowed steadily against the swift current, chanting a prayer to the upriver wind for favor.

The apprentice lay with eyes closed. That he was on the familiar way to Tu-To was a dream; in a moment he would find himself back in his own room near Dai's pigpen. His eyelids opened hastily for reassurance. Above him the sun rose in the heavens, and his chilled body began to relax. With interest he looked about. On either bank, small villages huddled under banyans and willows. Farmers cultivated their fields on slanting hillsides; fishermen cast outstretched nets close to shore. All was at peace; it was absurd to think of bandits.

One of the boatmen prepared the noon meal on a tiny charcoal stove. The soldiers ate heartily, demanding more than their share. They made it clear that they did not underestimate their value to the coppersmith on this journey. Tang accepted their attitude without comment.

At sunset they reached Tu-To. The coppersmith had friends in the town, and he sent a member of the crew ashore to invite them on board. In an hour or so they appeared and remained until midnight.

Young Fu spread his *pu-gai* on the deck and rolled himself in it. From where he lay he could see the maze of boat life surrounding them. An occasional lantern flickered from a bamboo rod; smoke and the flash of red embers rose from many cooking pans. Families moved about on decks, settling children and pigs and chickens for the night. One boatman, more daring than the rest, weighed anchor and turned in the dark toward Chungking. In the tiny cabin their own crew gambled at dominoes. Fragments of Tang's conversation with his Tu-To friends drifted to the boy's ears. The words "ban-keh" and "close by" came clearly. A flare from the fire showed the anxious expression of one who seemed to be arguing.

"You would be wise to send your things from here by the post," he said.

"That is why I came," replied Tang. "Has not the post been taken many times this past year?"

"Better lose the brasses than your life," warned another.

"Disaster falls on those who try hardest to avoid it!" quoted the coppersmith. "If it be Heaven's will for me to join the spirits of my ancestors at this time, there is no help for it."

Their voices lowered again and, lulled by the swaying of the boat, Young Fu fell asleep.

Stars were still flickering in the soft gray haze as they moved into midstream the next morning. To one accustomed to Chungking's early clamor, the hush about this smaller water front was startling. Young Fu stretched within his pu-gai, then lay still. This was the first time in his life that he had not jumped into action at the moment of waking. Each hour stolen from toil meant that much less rice in one's stomach. Sufficient sleep was something enjoyed by the rich and the priests only. Of course, there were certain days in the year—

New Year's, and spring and autumn festivals—when one had holiday from work, but no one would be so foolish as to waste those in sleeping.

A shadow broke in upon his thoughts. It was Tang, and the apprentice rose hastily.

"Do not hurry. There is no need for it. Save your strength for better work in the shop," the master suggested with a smile. "We are getting a good start," he continued, "and ought to reach Hochow soon after midday rice."

Bluffs formed an amphitheater about them; the water that dashed against the prow held a mossy tinge. This beauty must resemble that of the great gorges of the Yangtze below Chungking, the boy told himself. Some day, perhaps, he would see them too.

Aloud he said, "This land is good to look at."

Tang nodded briefly. His eyes clouded as he pointed to a blue hill in the distance. "There was I born and there I lived until I was your age. For twenty generations my ancestors were farmers on Smiling Heaven Hill. When I was sixteen, strife arose here in this province and it was the work of a few hours for looting soldiers to burn our possessions and kill my family. I, alone, was left. I escaped and made my way overland to Chungking, begging food as I went. There one day I stopped— like any street beggar—before the shop of Tu, the coppersmith. He refused me the cash I asked for, but gave me work to do. Later he taught me the trade. His heart was good!" Tang's voice ceased; he was lost in memories.

Young Fu felt a new loyalty. This was not merely the proprietor with whom he was familiar, but a human being who had eaten much bitterness. Together they walked over to the cook and reached for bowls of rice. The soldiers were grumbling over theirs, and the boy thought how deeply Tang must hate all of their profession.

At noon a shot whistled over their heads, then two more, then silence. The soldiers dropped to the floor of the boat; the crew missed a stroke, but rowed steadily on. Young Fu listened anxiously for a command to halt; none came. He looked at the others. Eyelids narrowed, Tang scanned the soft verdure of the closer bank. It betrayed nothing. The captain held the craft to her course and muttered to himself. The soldiers kept to their huddled position.

Two hours later, Hochow was sighted. Once ashore, carriers were summoned and the *mei-shiang-tz*, guarded by Tang and his apprentice, were soon deposited within the gateway of the government *ya-men*. After a brief wait they were ushered into a small reception room; Tang dismissed the carriers and Young Fu opened the baskets and placed the brasses, piece by piece, on a table for the three officials to examine. Murmurs of appreciation were heard with the display of each article, and the boy felt a thrill of pride over this work in which he had had a part. This, he discovered for himself, meant more to Tang than would the payment in money. Personal pride in the quality of his work was the highest return any craftsman might ask.

One of the mandarins spoke, "Peking is my native place. There have I seen many fine specimens of such work, but nothing more beautiful than these before me."

Tang bowed low. He regretted that he had been forced by lack of time to present such undesirable examples of brass cutting to their honorable attention, he told them in reply, but his eyes could not conceal his satisfaction.

The afternoon passed swiftly. The brasses were settled for in Szechuen silver, after which tea was served. Then, with much bowing and many courteous phrases from both sides, Tang and Young Fu made their way back to the boat. Crew and soldiers had gone ashore, only the captain remained. In an hour the three of them were asleep.

The next morning the boy was awakened by the sound of Tang's voice raised in anger. The soldiers had not yet returned from their night ashore, and the captain, with the advantage of a strong down-river wind, hoped by making an early start to reach Chungking at nightfall. A member of the crew was sent to inquire along the water front for the missing men, but the errand proved fruitless. Without further hesitation, Tang gave the order to cast off. No one had any doubts but that the soldiers had been frightened by the previous day's warning shots.

As they rushed along with the current, Young Fu wondered what would happen, now that the silver was aboard, if the *ban-keh* should order them to halt. No one was armed, and his memory recalled some of the ugly tales current in Chungking about the fate of captives who attempted to save their goods or themselves. He glanced at Tang, whose responsibility the matter was. That worthy seemed lighter hearted than at any time on the journey. Young Fu smiled and shrugged his shoulders. There was no need for carrying his worry in his hand.

The day was nearing its close when the boatman pointed to a change of sky. Darkness hastening from every direction closed in upon them suddenly. The stiff breeze which had pushed them all day long over the surface of the water as suddenly died. The crew pulled at the oars. An occasional drop of rain carried sinister warning. Tang and the captain conferred earnestly. The latter gave an order, and the boat was steered into a small cove to the right.

As they cast anchor in this shelter, the clouds burst. The sky was now pitch black, but no one dared to light a lantern. Only four miles away was Chungking and safety; here in this lonely spot the possibility of danger so thickened the air that breathing became momentarily more difficult. No one spoke. Shivering with cold, they waited only for the storm to abate, but there seemed no end to the rain. The boatmen crowded into the tiny cabin, and Tang and the boy squatted with the captain under a temporary shelter of matting at the stern. The Szechuen silver, tied securely in two heavy squares of unbleached muslin, rested behind the coppersmith's feet. Young Fu's eyes wandered in the darkness to where he knew it lay. His flesh crept. The cold metal, in this period of delay, assumed undue power for evil.

He shifted his position, pushing an uncomfortable pile of matting strips and odd rags from under him. As he did so, the little boat lurched wildly. A screech rang out from the farther end of the craft. There was a mad scuffling of feet and yells of pain. Someone screamed, "*Ban-keh! Ban-keh!*" A gruff voice rose above the bedlam and demanded the captain.

Young Fu's heart thudded; his skin turned to goose flesh. Five—ten—seconds elapsed, and then like a flash it came to him what to do. He not only knew where to hide the silver; he would hide himself as well! Without his presence, Tang could pass as an ordinary traveler, rather than as a successful merchant with an apprentice. A whisper, and Tang understood. He took the captain into the scheme and together they worked madly the remaining seconds before a torch flared over their end of the boat. When it did, it disclosed Tang and the captain crouched beneath a shelter of matting.

Two of the bandits guarded the crew, two held torches, while the fifth figure was evidently in command. He pushed forward.

Tang rose to his feet. "Is there anything I can do for you?" he inquired pleasantly.

"Who are you?"

"The passenger on this boat, and a citizen of Chungking."

"What is your business anchored here?"

"Refuge from the tubsful of water being emptied on us from above."

"A likely tale! From what place did you come?"

"Hochow."

"Your business there?"

"Paying reverence to ancestral tablets."

The other glared at him suspiciously. His glance swept from captain to crew. "Is what he says true?" he barked.

Under Tang's watchful eye they nodded solemnly.

"Search all of them!" the chief ordered.

Little was found on the crew. The captain and Tang contributed the most, a trifle over eight dollars.

Young Fu, smothering beneath the heap of rags and matting at the side of the boat, hoped the affair would soon be settled. Anxiously he listened while the bandit spoke. "This is not enough," the gruff voice said. "You look prosperous for one with so little money. With what did you intend to pay this boatman?"

The reply came without hesitation, "A Chungking check."

"Give me the check."

"You have it in your hand—that torn scrap of paper."

The bandit looked at it wonderingly. It was plain he had not seen one before. He turned to the torchbearer. "Is this a bank check?" he asked.

The man admitted that he did not know.

One of the other guards came forward. After careful examination of the slip, he assured the chief that, if

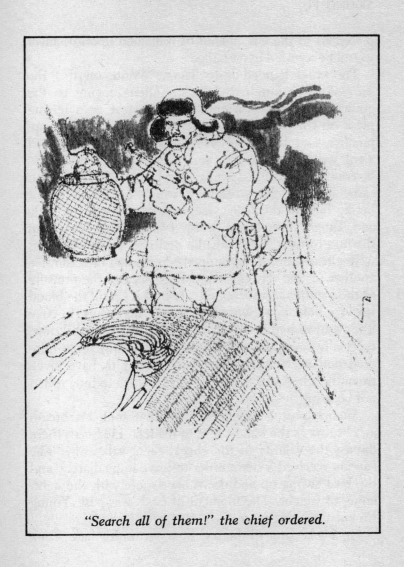

"Search all of them!" the chief ordered.

presented to the Chungking bank named upon it, silver would be received in exchange.

The chief handed it to Tang. "Write on this the sum of three hundred dollars." Then moving to the gunwale, he sat down and lifted his feet to a resting place on the pile of rags under which the shivering apprentice and the silver lay hidden, while he watched Tang write the characters for three hundred dollars.

Young Fu flattened against the boat floor. His breath came in short gasps, each of which he feared might betray him to the heavy feet separated from his body and Tang's silver by so flimsy a protection. Dirt from the rags tortured him with the desire to sneeze. His legs were already numb. A cramped hip seemed unendurable another second. He felt faint. Each second the pressure of the bandit's feet increased. He bit his lip till the blood ran, to hold consciousness. So far his effort to save Tang's silver had been successful. He must not fail now, especially since the coppersmith was losing three hundred dollars. It would have been better to have given them the silver at the first. If only the idea to hide it had not been his!

An unexpected weight of pain that took his breath away came as the bandit rose to his feet. He heard them discuss the validity of the check, then walk away. The captain received a sharp order to leave immediately, and the boat swung up and down once more with the lightening of weight. The moment of crisis was past. Young Fu knew nothing more.

He awoke later to the feel of water on his face. Tang

knelt beside him, chafing his hands, feeling his body for injuries. They were moving swiftly down the river. The rain had ceased, and overhead the clouds were breaking. The crew rowed madly—all were scared to death.

Young Fu raised himself painfully to a sitting posture. He was stiff and sore, and his mind was heavy. If only he had not been so hot-hearted to manage the affair. Tang would never keep him after this. Vanished in a moment were all his dreams of becoming a great craftsman. As for his mother—!

The coppersmith interrupted this unpleasant thinking: "You have courage. It is as I said, you have no fear of devils and they do not notice you. You have saved me much silver tonight. I shall not soon forget it."

Young Fu turned the words over in his brain. Tang was not angry. What did it mean?

"But the check—" He did not know how to finish.

"The check was worthless. It bore the name of a small bank that for lack of funds closed its front more than a year ago. When I saw that scrap of paper mixed with my money in the *ban-keh*'s hand, the idea came to try to trick them. It was a risk, but they were stupid."

The boy's relief was overwhelming. His eyes stung with an unusual mist. So he had not been foolish after all. He might have trusted Tang to see the scheme through.

In the sky there was no trace of previous storm. Chungking's shadowy gray walls were etched softly by starlight. Soon he would be with Fu Be Be, relating the adventure to her startled ears.

Tang spoke again: "Fortune smiled on us. Those bandits are new to such business, of that I am sure. The experienced ones are not so easily satisfied. Moreover, they were light of hand. You suffered more harm than anyone else."

His apprentice rubbed sore ribs. "Ai!" he agreed with a rueful smile, "their strength lay in their feet!"

A
RIVER
ON THE
RAMPAGE

He could not wait to tell Small Li of his experience. This was an affair in which all was to his credit and Li, given time, would see to it that the shop in general and Small Den in particular heard the story. Later, some sense of dignity made him happy that he had not found it necessary to relate an incident so complimentary to himself. On his arrival at the shop the next morning, Tang accosted him. "Do your bones still ache?" In another moment the coppersmith was launched on an account of all that had happened.

Small Li was thrilled. "I told you bandits would find you!"

"You were wrong. They do not yet know that I was on the boat."

Small Den standing to one side curled his lip. "To look like a bundle of rags must have been easy for the countryman."

Young Fu flushed with anger. He turned in Den's direction only to hear Tang say, "Everyone to work! We have spent enough time in talk."

In another moon Den's apprenticeship, Young Fu consoled himself, would be at an end, and he hoped devoutly that the other would pass out of his life. That Den irked the coppersmith, all in the place recognized, and Tang was not likely to insist on his remaining as a journeyman. There was nothing remarkable about Den's work with metal. He had, however, all of the qualifications for a clever clerk. His fingers manipulated the beads of the abacus more swiftly than did the accountant's, and in his reckoning mistakes were rare. Den had learned, as well, the handful of characters essential to the keeping of books, and, young as he was, he could with his supercilious air awe more than one customer into purchasing what he wished them to buy.

The end of Li's term would follow Den's and, in turn,

his own. To begin, his wages would be small, but, with care, a living could be provided for two.

Den's day of freedom came and passed and with it Den himself. Wu, Tang's chief competitor, had invited the newly released apprentice to figure accounts for him. When Den and all his belongings had disappeared from sight, Old Tsu voiced his feelings, "A bird of evil omen has flown from the rooftree!"

Tang shrugged his shoulders. "Even upon Wu I would not have wished such ill fortune."

A new apprentice, named Feng, came to take Den's place. He was homely of countenance and seemed stupid. Young Fu joined with the others in teasing the newcomer, until the memory of his own miserable first day smote him. When the men had returned to work, he sought out the stranger. "Lay down your heart," he said, looking into the sullen face that lifted to his, "what you have had to bear today is shared commonly by all new apprentices. Never shall I forget my first meal here, but this is a good place to work and," warmth crept into his voice, "there is no better master in Chungking than Tang."

Young Fu recalled this conversation the following day as he compared the early duties of his own apprenticeship with the important tasks to which he was now assigned. Early in the afternoon, Tang had sent him off alone with a valuable order for an official in the Chungking hills. The delivery had been made and signed for, and he now sat on the river bank awaiting some possible means of transport. A boatload of eggplants finally appeared, and after bargaining with its owner for passage, he paid his fare and sat on the gunwale.

A stiff wind was blowing, and though the almanac foretold the approach of spring, the biting air and scudding clouds were evidence enough that winter's bitter lips had not yet closed. As the boatman pushed out against the current, a wave higher than the rest lifted them up, and in a moment a dozen purple globules from the boat's contents had slipped into the water and were bobbing about like so many porpoises.

"Catch them! Catch them!" commanded the man, struggling to pole his craft over the rapidly roughening surface of the river.

Young Fu obeyed. The sky was darkening and he had an uneasy feeling that the hour was later than he had thought. He must have been a long time on that river bank, and if they did not reach the other side soon, he would find the city gates closed for the night. Nine wet eggplants were retrieved before the boatman, grumbling over his loss, turned once more toward the Chungking shore.

As they touched land, Young Fu leaped out, raced madly across the mud, climbed the long flights of steps leading to the gateway and knocked for entrance. Beyond the strong, barred partition echoed the clamor of the city's life; here, several hundred feet above the shore, a curtain of silence fused with the evening mists. He pounded again and again on the gate, but no answer came; and finally his tired arms sank in dejection to his sides. The effort was of no use—he was too late, and not one of the many doorways set in Chungkings's ancient wall would, now that dusk was falling, swing open to let him in.

There was nothing to do but face a night outside the city. In itself this was no particular calamity. His chief worry was Fu Be Be. His mother knew nothing of his errand, and Tang did not expect him to return to the shop until the following morning. She would be sure the worst had happened. Aside from that responsibility, with several coppers in his belt bestowed on him by the customer in the hills, he rather welcomed this new experience of spending one night where thousands of Chungking's population spent their lives.

If one were so poor that time fell naturally into two periods, when one ate and when one did not, or if one had any of a hundred diseases and deformities, a flimsy shelter raised on stilts above the mud flats was more easily acquired than a like protection within the city, where men paid dearly for all benefits. Also, the sharp-sighted and the agile found it less difficult to pick up food here than elsewhere. Fruit and vegetable boats plied incessantly on the Yangtze, and the River Dragon could be counted upon to steal something from each load and cast it up with the waves. He had his good moments—the River Dragon—and when he wreaked mischief on the ferrymen, the inhabitants of the mud flats gained by his playfulness. True, he had other moods. There came a night at the end of each winter— but wisdom counseled silence on such thinking. This was the time of year when his disposition seemed worst, and men would be fools to put ideas into his head.

So thought Old Mother Ling as she sat on a small stool before her mud hut on the river bank, and watched the swirling flood with ominous eyes. The *Hsien-Seng*, her husband, had gone to the pawn shop to see if their summer garments were still secure and to inquire whether the winter ones were considered of sufficient value to redeem the others when the time came. Warm weather would be a matter of several weeks hence, but with a pawn shop one could never tell. In the past, before wars had ruined them, Mother Ling and the *Hsien-Seng* had had no dealings with such places. Today, however! The old lady sighed, rose from the stool, and entered the hut.

Young Fu, crossing the flats toward her, called out as he reached the door, "*Lao-Po-Po!*"

The little figure reappeared and he changed his mode of address to "*Si-Mu.*" Certainly this old grandmother with her clean clothes and smooth hair bore no relationship to the coolie women who lived all about her.

"What do you wish?" she asked him.

"I am late, *Si-Mu*, from an errand to the hills—too late to enter the city. I am hungry and must sleep. Would you permit me to purchase with dishonorable coins a share of your evening rice and the protection of your dwelling?"

The sharp old eyes looked into the bright ones facing her. "There are public places, even in this wretched district," she said.

"I know, Respected Lady, but they do not tempt me. That I am a stranger is true, but lay down your heart, I am apprenticed to Tang, the coppersmith, and I do not have dirty fingers!"

Mother Ling smiled ruefully, "Even if you did, there would be nothing in this house for you to steal. However, there is food and, while it is of poor quality, you shall share it with us—but not for money."

Soon afterward her husband joined them. Young Fu again explained his plight and the old man listened attentively.

"What are the signs of spring in the hills?" he asked.

"The rice spears cut the surface of the pools and azalea shoots are rich with life. The farmers say that if the soldiers will interest themselves elsewhere for a few weeks, crops will be abundant."

"Ai! that is the problem," said Father Ling. "Soldiers! Always soldiers! The soil of this province is rich and farmers are ever ready to work. War is the curse of this land." He shook his head. "War drove us from Smiling Heaven Hill to this!" His eyelids drooped wearily. After a moment he whispered to himself, "Character is made by rising above one's misfortunes."

Young Fu's thoughts were on the trip with Tang to Hochow. Smiling Heaven Hill was the place Tang had pointed out as the home of his ancestors. He must remember to tell the coppersmith about this old couple.

Mother Ling interrupted, "Food is ready." They went within.

Later she gave her guest a comfort. He rolled up in it

on the earthen floor and was soon asleep. Father Ling, lost in memories, wrapped his own comfort around him and he, too, slipped into that other land of dreams.

The old lady huddled over the dying embers in her tiny charcoal stove. There were only two covers and they were both in use. She dozed fitfully. Her body was cramped from the sitting posture and cold. She moved her small bound feet about in the effort to increase circulation.

The *Hsien-Seng*, her husband, had whispered that their garments were safe. He had been pleased to remark so much virtue in the world. From season to season the pawn-shop proprietor had held their clothes for them, when who knew what offers he might have received! He was an honorable man! Her husband was always recognizing virtue in people. She herself knew their garments were so worn that it was unlikely anyone would wish to take them off the proprietor's hands. On the other side —loyalty welled within her—it was possible that the pawn-shop keeper had his own way of respecting superiority as represented in the *Hsien-Seng*. However, these garments would not last forever, and what of the future? What her husband earned by writing occasional letters for passersby at the nearest city gate barely bought food to keep them alive. Life was difficult!

A sudden strange roaring reached her ears. Startled, she strained to listen. Her breath shortened. She rose softly and went to the doorway. There, terror held her transfixed. Fifty yards away, the river, a mountainous wall of water, boiled and surged; broke and broke again, casting an ever-higher line of foam upon the mud. Her darkest fears of the afternoon had come true. The Dragon, choked by a surfeit of melting snows from peaks high above, had chosen this night for his annual display of temper. And men, always at his mercy, would either flee or fall within his cruel, grasping reach. Flee, the Dragon jeered; where could men flee outside the Chungking wall except to him?

Mother Ling, shaking herself free of his sinister spell, went trembling within. In a second she had roused and warned the others.

The three of them stood shivering and watched the danger come ever nearer. The two old people looked about in dismay. There was no place to go. At this rate the river would soon be lapping hungrily close to the Chungking wall. In another quarter of an hour their own hut would have disappeared—and they with it. They might just as well compose themselves to meet their fate.

But their youthful companion had no idea of being drowned if he could avoid it. His voice stirred them from their daze.

"Tie your most precious possessions together quickly and follow me!" he ordered. "On the Lin River side there is an ascent less steep than elsewhere, which leads to the back of the foreign buildings. Since the foreigners' hospital burned, the wall at that point has remained broken; once we are up the hillside, we may enter the city, I believe. And even if the wall should prove too high for climbing, the river will not be able to reach us there."

Mother Ling stumbled into the hut. She returned, pushing the two rolled comforts before her and carrying in her hand a small blue cloth in which reposed her few treasures.

The *Hsien-Seng* protested. "We cannot take the bedding. To climb the hillside to the wall will use all of our strength."

For once his wife refused to heed his wisdom. "Without the comforts we perish with cold. If we may not carry them, I will not go!" and she planted herself stubbornly on the stool.

Young Fu gasped. Every second was precious. The hissing flood had already gained several feet. There was no time for argument; this old grandmother was quite as capable as his own mother of keeping to a decision. He caught up the bedding and lifted it to his shoulders, then, motioning to his companions to hurry, he led the way.

The mud flats were a bedlam of sound. Human screams mingled with the cries of terrified animals. People were scrambling madly up the hillside, pulling their household possessions after them. Others were dismantling the bamboo walls of their homes and using the material to improvise rafts. Piling themselves and their possessions on these, they launched the shaky crafts on the bosom of the flood. Down on the lower levels the crippled and diseased lay helpless. Young Fu made his way through the weaving mass, and kept a sharp lookout for the place where he hoped to climb the wall. At last he sighted it, then waited for the old people to catch up with him. Fifteen feet away the river seethed. Fowls were floating on its surface. Furniture bobbed about. A body—! He shivered and faced the hillside quickly.

As he did so, Father and Mother Ling reached his side. Up over the rocky face of the cliff their leader climbed, trying to pick a path on which the others might tread. He had youth and strength and this was a hard business even for him. If it were not for these comforts, he could help the old lady. But the others were struggling bravely to follow him. He propped his bundle against a bramble root and wiped the sweat from his face. When they had caught up to him, he permitted them a few minutes rest, and then started on.

Twenty feet higher he halted again. The founders of Chungking had been wise to build it on its rocky promontory. An enemy would think twice before attempting to scale this hillside, even if no sentinels watched from the wall above. At this point he helped the old people to a rest on the roll of bedding. Their faces and hands were scratched and bruised; their garments torn; Mother Ling's shoes shredded. She was biting her lips in pain; through them her breath came in gasps.

Young Fu encouraged them: "Here we are almost beyond the river's reach, but we must go on. Cold and dampness out under the moon would accomplish what the River Dragon has failed to do. Once in the city, we shall have food and warmth." He picked up his load.

The journey was a nightmare of such climbs and rests. The old people were becoming momentarily more exhausted. Young Fu felt bruised and beaten. Horror lay

Horror lay below them.

below them. As the victims of the river's wrath fought to escape, their shrieks pierced even the roar of water. Years seemed to have passed before he could touch the city wall.

A voice called and a lantern swung its light over them. "Who are you?"

Young Fu explained. In another moment, the man, a servant in the foreign house, had scaled the barrier. Together, he and Young Fu helped the two others over and, in turn, led them within. Young Fu brightened in recognition as the woman with yellow hair appeared.

She looked surprised to see him. "What have you been doing tonight—cheating another dragon of its prey?" she asked with a smile. Then she turned to the old people. Now that the hospital patients were all lodged in this house, things were crowded, but there was a little room where the two refugees might stay until they recovered from their recent ordeal.

Young Fu thanked her and the *Hsien-Seng* bowed his appreciation. But Mother Ling, for the first time, began to whimper. She had never had dealings with foreigners and she was afraid to remain in this house. Her husband apologized for her timidity, then, leaning over, whispered gently in her ear. When he was assured that there would be no more trouble, Young Fu promised to visit them the next day and left for home.

He found his mother huddled on the door sill. At the sight of him she began to scold fiercely, then, weakening, sobbed out her relief. Later she listened to his story, cared for his bruises, and helped him into bed.

At Tang's the next morning they teased him about his scratched face and hands. "Did you meet a devil?" asked Li.

"Truly! I was without the wall last night."

Led on by their satisfying interest, he related the experience. Accounts of last night's damage had been coming to them indirectly. Here was one of their own who had been there in person. They gathered about him.

Tang turned an amused glance toward the hero of the hour. "Did you dream this?" he inquired.

"No! Moreover, these people bear the surname Ling, and they once lived on Smiling Heaven Hill near Tu-To."

The coppersmith came nearer. "Our closest neighbor and my father's best friend was named Ling." Then he disposed of the thought with a gesture. "He was no coolie who dwelt on mud flats!"

"Neither is this man a coolie. He reminds me of Wang Scholar. Also, he said that war had caused his misfortune."

Tang's thoughts turned to the past. Thirty-four years ago! He could see his father sitting in their reception room drinking tea with his neighbor. From the bowls of their long pipes drifted thin spirals of smoke. The neighbor had a taste for the Classics. Phrases from their conversation came to him dimly. He had been a lad of sixteen when left for dead by the soldiers who had killed his family and burned his home. Their neighbors, he had supposed, had all fared as badly. He turned to his apprentice.

"Where are these people now?" he inquired.

"At the foreign woman's. Today, after work is finished, I go to pay my respects." Young Fu rubbed a smutty hand over his forehead in embarrassment at his feeling of pity. "They are old and poor, but they lacked not courage."

"You will go as soon as I speak to Lu about this morning's orders," contradicted Tang, "and I will go with you."

They found the old lady propped up in bed, delighting in the attention she was receiving from nurses. Her husband was occupied happily in reading aloud to other patients. His eyes lighted at Young Fu's appearance.

"We owe you much," he told the youth simply. Then he bowed in greeting to Tang. Suddenly his expression changed, as his eyes fastened on the coppersmith's face. At last he spoke.

"Excuse me, sir," he said, "you resemble someone I knew in former years whose excellent surname was the same as yours. But I am an old man and my memory confuses dreams with realities."

Tang moved closer. "Was the one you remember, Ancient One, your neighbor? And in the long evenings did you talk and smoke together?"

The *Hsien-Seng's* hands were trembling. "We did," he whispered, "and you are Tang Yu-hsu's youngest son!"

Tang smiled. "You speak truly. You, Venerable Sir, were my father's closest friend."

Young Fu watched wide-eyed while Tang helped the

older man to a seat. Yesterday's overexertion and today's shock were too much for even the *Hsien-Seng*'s self-control. After a time the two men lost themselves in quiet conversation.

The apprentice slipped through the doorway to the back wall. There he climbed the broken stones and looked below. The shore was strewn with wreckage. Hundreds of yesterday's tenements had disappeared and many of their tenants would not again be seen. The river was still swollen, but in the sunlight it presented a sparkling surface. Now that the Dragon's anger had been appeased it would, for today, assume its most beguiling mood and coax these helpless little men creatures to play with it again.

Young Fu thought of its treachery and searched for the spot where he had seen Mother Ling first enter her door. A clear space without sign of habitation met his eye. It was a relief to think of them now safe in the foreign house. And they would not again have to worry about the future—Tang would see to that. For one household, at least, the Dragon had been forced to admit defeat. Dragons! He sniffed to himself. After all it was simply a matter of keeping one's head and outwitting them! With a gaminish gesture of derision toward the river, he turned his back and stepped forward. It might be good for him to remind Tang, by a sudden appearance, that there were important affairs awaiting them at the shop.

A
SMALL
PROBLEM
OF
OWNERSHIP

TEN DAYS LATER, Small Li's apprenticeship expired, and he became an accepted journeyman at Tang's. Li's parents acknowledged the importance of the occasion by giving a feast to their son's fellow workers. The newly appointed artisan elected to sleep under his own roof, and still another apprentice came to fill his position and bed at the shop.

In his elevated rank of journeyman, Li finished the day usually before Young Fu's duties were at an end. Several times he waited for his young friend, but his mother, annoyed by this delay in serving evening rice, soon put a stop to this practice. At work the two friends had little time for talk and they missed the companionship which errands had given them.

There was, in these days, much to talk about. The Nationalist Government, true to its promise, was spending money in Chungking. To the deep consternation of most of the older people, men had torn down the Land Gate to Dsen-Gia-Ngai, leaving an exposed, unprotected section of wall for the first time in Chungking's history.

The graybeards shook their heads. "With the Land Gate open to the world, what defense have we?" they wished to know.

No one listened. Instead, a broad, smooth roadway lengthened itself from the city gate to the main highways of travel. Ten sedan chairs might have passed abreast on it had they wished. The carts of which the Hankow man had first told Tang now appeared. Great lumbering vehicles they were, into which a few daring souls stepped for the initial ride. All of Chungking that was able turned out to witness the spectacle.

Young Fu received Tang's permission to pass that way on another errand. The chauffeur started his engine. Its first roar terrified the crowd. Women screamed but nothing happened. The engine sputtered and became silent;

the motor bus stood in exactly the same spot. The crowd's fear was lost in hilarious amusement.

"Are my eyes bad," jeered one of the old men, "that I still see this devil-machine? Or has it been to Dsen-Gia-Ngia and returned?"

Again the engine roared, coughed sickeningly, and died. The onlookers became hilarious. "Mo's chair shop is close by. Shall we call ten bearers from there to pull your cart for you?"

The embarrassed driver alighted, lifted the engine hood, and with a practiced finger poked about while the crowd pressed in on him.

"Ai-ya! look at the queer thing!"

"What fools men are to believe that a piece of iron and some lengths of pipe can run like a donkey!"

"Where does it hide its legs?"

Satisfied, the chauffeur covered the engine, slipped into his leather seat, and ordered the frightened passengers once more aboard. In another moment the bus had moved startlingly away.

The spectators rubbed their eyes as a cloud of dust sifted back to them. The sound of the motor reached them ever more faintly. They stood in a daze. It could not be possible that this spirit-machine had actually gone without assistance.

Miracles did not stop with this innovation. A building in which another devil-engine was chained rose in the city. The sound of its angry voice was constant, as it pumped water into tanks for those who could afford to pay for it. The liquid was said to be cleaner than that

which the water coolies dipped directly from the river.
But Chungking's streets became no less slippery than
they had been. As yet only the well-to-do had money to
pay for such service.

When her son mentioned it, Fu Be Be shrugged her
shoulders. "Had I much silver I would not wish this
water. There is something queer about sucking up the
River Dragon's bed in this fashion. Evil is certain to
come of it."

Young Fu smiled tolerantly. "The foreigners fear no
Dragons—nor do I"—he paused to moderate this statement—"very greatly."

"The foreigners! The foreigners! Like a monkey you
copy their ways! Are you no longer able to think as did
your forefathers? Little would they have had to do with
these foreigners."

"My ancestors did not know these foreigners, and I,
who am ten-tenths Chinese, do. From them I have had
only kindness. The foreign woman was grateful for the
service that I did her as one of our own race might have
been grateful. Money she sent me; trade she has since
given Tang; Small Li's life was saved when he would
otherwise have died; the old people found shelter in her
house."

"Men die at the appointed time. Small Li's hour had
not struck. Your foreigner receives the credit. Perhaps,"
she granted him with a generous air, "the yellow-haired
woman is not like the others; even tigers differ in their
stripes and whiskers."

Young Fu glimpsed a flicker of amusement in his

mother's eye and responded to it with a laugh. Such conversations were becoming more and more common between them, and it was well to have them end lightly whenever possible. Fu Be Be, like most of the mothers and grandmothers, found it difficult to believe in the good of anything new. Wang Scholar, lost in contemplation of the Classics, paid little attention to what was happening about him. Tang missed nothing; usually he reserved his opinion until a fair judgment could be made. But that life was changing all around them, Young Fu told himself, there was no doubt.

Soldiers no longer loafed in tea houses. Often groups of them in brisk action passed him on the street, their minds engrossed in their own affairs. Builders were tearing down rows of old houses in the business districts and erecting tall, foreign structures of strange design.

The new government's strength was being proved on all sides. Men who had doubted it most now began to discuss it with confidence. That it had enemies as active as itself, Young Fu did not realize until he peered one evening through the wedge of human bodies that blocked the entrance to Abiding Delight Tea House. Within, a young man stood on a table and denounced the foreigners, the ways of rotten generals, and, most hotly of all, the government at Nanking.

The audience, entertained for the moment by something new, listened, smiled occasionally at one another, and said nothing. And it was argument, not silence, that the speaker desired, Young Fu said in his mind; otherwise he would not hurl so many questions that demanded answers. One by one these inquiries sank into the pool of indifference surrounding the young man as he waited, eyes sparkling with displeasure, then concluded vehemently: "For this reason, Workers of the World, are you oppressed. You bend your backs willingly to the burdens your masters, the rich and powerful, press upon them! You speak no word of complaint! Whether you spend your strength to seize that which is rightfully yours, or whether you continue as slaves and your children as slaves, is your affair. To show men the way to freedom is ours. If they will not heed, that is their loss!" He jumped from his position of vantage, moved to an empty seat, and bawled an order for tea.

Young Fu smiled. This fellow's temper was fired by lack of appreciation—a bad business for one trying to teach a new doctrine. Wang Scholar had a saying, "No man can rule the unruly until he first rules himself." The truth of this statement this young man did not recognize.

The crowd decided that no more entertainment offered itself, and melted gradually into the stream of traffic passing the tea house. Young Fu lingered to study the speaker. The latter's manner of speaking the Chungking dialect was foreign. He was shorter in stature than was the average Chungkingese and he affected tan leather shoes and a foreign hair cut. Perhaps the young man was from the South, but if that were so, he would not be talking against the Southern government.

A farmer walked over to where the object of this scrutiny sat sipping tea, and began to ask questions. From Young Fu's footing against the carved framework of the

"For this reason are you oppressed."

shop entrance, he could distinguish nothing that was said, until the stranger's voice rose in excitement: "When your crops fail, pay no rent! Should your landlord eat when your own rice bowl is empty? In that day when land shall belong to all, crops will be shared equally; no man will have more than another. Take from the rich and give to the poor—that is our doctrine. Only in that way will the world become free."

The farmer looked startled. He bowed his thanks, then made his way to the front where he stood in indecision, wriggling the straw sandal cords between his bare toes. Rakishly, an onlooker nudged him. "Pay no rent! Take Landlord Dsong's land from him! You will soon be rich."

The other shook his head. "It is a wild doctrine," he said. "Landlord Dsong does not cause drought. And I do not want too many to own the land on which I work. Affairs are bad enough as they are. Nor do I wish to share the fruits of my toil with my neighbors. Does T'sen, who plants two crops a year in the field adjoining mine, deserve as much as I who spend effort in cultivating five?" Muttering to himself, he wandered down the street and Young Fu soon followed him.

"Why so late?" Fu Be Be demanded when he reached home.

"I halted at Abiding Delight Tea House."

"For one so young, to have time and money to spend in tea houses is certainly unusual. I congratulate you on your excellent fortune!"

Mockingly her son replied, "I am most unworthy,

Honorable Parent, of your courtesies. I stopped merely to listen for a few minutes to a man from far away, whose heart was excited over many matters."

"The shallow teapot does the most spouting, and boils dry most quickly!"

"This man had not boiled dry. He would have talked forever had anyone remained to hear. He wished the poor to steal treasure from the rich and keep it for themselves."

Fu Be Be's tongue clicked. "The prattle of babes! That has always been the ambition of the lazy."

Settling down to work at the coppersmith's the next morning, Old Tsu halted long enough to ask of the other workmen, "Why do these strangers at present in this city talk to artisans and farmers whose hands are busy from dawn to dark? It would be better for them to spend their breath on the rich—they have time to heed." He chuckled to himself. "These most recent agitators, I understand, come from the South. Are their own districts so perfect that nothing remains to be done there?"

The others nodded their heads knowingly, then moved away to take up the day's tasks. Only Wei stood still, his eyes smoldering in resentment, his lips opening to speak, then closing firmly. After a pause, he, too, picked up a piece of work.

Young Fu, pretending to examine a sheet of copper, watched him. This man, Wei, was a puzzle. In coming to fill Dsen's place, he had proved his ability as a workman, but had antagonized all of his associates. From the first his dissatisfaction had been evident. He had, when-

ever Tang's back was turned, complained of many things
—the poor wages, the cheap food that was served, the
long hours of toil, and Tang's increasing prosperity. The
other workmen had listened to these tirades without
comment; an occasional knowing smile or wink showed
the boy how they felt toward this newcomer. Suddenly
it occurred to him that what Wei had to say usually was
much like the speech he had heard in the tea house.
That speaker must have been one of the political agitators mentioned by Old Tsu, and perhaps Wei was
another.

In the afternoon, Young Fu set out with some samples of stock to one of the foreign business houses. Returning, he found a mob blocking the entrance to the
home of Su, a wealthy official. Voices were shouting,
"Kill the rich! Divide their possessions!"

Furniture lay strewn about the courtyard, and clothing was being thrown from every opening. Among the
two or three strangers who seemed to be managing the
affair was the tea-house speaker. Su's servants stood helpless in the rear of the compound, while coolies from the
street rushed about selecting what loot appealed to their
eyes. Two of Su's children clung to an amah who
guarded them jealously. The older boy's face was ashy
with fear; the younger cried openly. Su and the women
of the household were nowhere to be seen. Young Fu
heard someone say that Su was not in the city. It was
possible he had taken his three wives with him. The
youth slipped away from the crowd. Certainly soldiers

would end this affair promptly, and it was the part of wisdom to leave before they arrived.

Later, when he repeated the tale to the workmen, their faces expressed varying degrees of amazement. Wei laughed. "Fortune is just! Su's father was a scavenger— had his son not turned bandit, he would have followed that trade, is it not so? Instead, having acquired much money, he becomes an important man in this city. What was taken from him today once belonged to others. It is good that it be returned."

"Perhaps," replied Tang. "That Su is a rotten egg all men know, but that wrongs should be mended in that fashion is for me a question. It is not likely that the coolies who were given Su's treasures today were robbed in the past by his *ban-keh*."

Wei said nothing else. He seemed, however, to find his thoughts amusing.

That night one of the foreign houses was looted and its occupants beaten. Young Fu could not wait to reach the shop the next morning. As he had expected, Wei's voice rose above the other sounds, "We shall not stop until every foreigner has left the shores of the Middle Kingdom. They are our worst enemies, and their armies wait for the chance to make us slaves."

Young Fu thought of the foreign woman. Was she, also, an enemy? She spent her days healing the sick. This was puzzling. Tang's next remark to Wei drew back his wavering attention. "The world knows no lack of men who would change its ways, neither does the

Middle Kingdom suffer from such a loss. And recently I have heard it said that Chinese and foreigner alike smile on this doctrine of yours. Why then denounce those who are at one with you?"

Wei reddened. "I do not understand you," he muttered. "I am a son of Han and I would save this country for the Black-haired People."

"I, also," said Tang. "But it has been our custom to think out our own systems of government. Why borrow ideas from outsiders? I waste no time saying foolish things about the foreigners—that is simply to blind ourselves to what is wrong in our own house. Neither do I ask their wisdom or their strength. Have we no longer thinkers and men of ability left in the land?"

"You, naturally, would say nothing against the foreigners—they buy your brasses."

"A fact," retorted Tang, "which does not seal my lips. There are several kinds of foreigners, as there are of Middle Kingdom men. Some have good hearts. Some I like so little I care not who kills them. But to declare that they have brought all of the evils from which this land suffers, is the talk of fools!"

"The day will come when you will not dare to say that!" threatened Wei, his voice hot with anger.

"Truly?" Tang smiled as though humoring a child. "I will wait until that time comes to carry my heart in my hand. Begin your work!"

Wei threw down the piece of brass he had been holding. It clattered over the hard-baked floor. "Who are you to order me to work?" he demanded.

Young Fu's heart jumped. He stooped and picked up the kettle as it rolled to his feet. This was no way to speak to the master of an establishment.

Tang was staring steadily at the other man. "I am the head of this place," he informed him. "If you do not like my commands, you may go." He turned to the clerk. "Reckon this man's account and pay him at once!"

As Wei passed into the street, Old Tsu whispered, "That should have happened the day he arrived."

A week of confusion passed. The disturbing element increased its activities daily. Most of the foreigners had fled to the gunboat in the Big River; much of their property had been ruined. In the shop the men shook their heads gravely. War they were used to, and looting, where all suffered equally, they could understand. But with these so-called reformers, no one knew who would receive the next blow. Anyone might be the victim of their fever to change the social order.

Wang Scholar looked on the world with somber eyes. One evening he stood with Young Fu on the door sill of Dai's house. "My heart fails under the burden of this land," he said. "Neither the wisdom of the sages nor the experience of centuries helps us. Generals come long enough to loot or to levy taxes, then leave us for the grasping fingers of their successors. We are like a fowl from whose bones even the marrow has been sucked."

"As for these present agitators," the old teacher shook his head, "more than three thousand years ago our countrymen shared wisely and with loving hearts, their land and wealth. The Sons of Heaven, our rulers, ordered

171

all as it should be, and the nation prospered." He sighed. "But men have departed from the ways of the ancients, and the new ones leave only misery in their path."

At the coppersmith's, the problem of political disorder assumed secondary importance to a more personal matter. Old Tsu's youngest son was to be married, and the father invited everyone at Tang's to the feast. Expanding in hospitality, he told the two new apprentices that they also might go to his house and play with his grandchildren.

Tang held the gay red-paper invitation in his hand and lost himself in thought. He walked over to Young Fu. "Do you wish greatly to attend this wedding feast?"

"Why?"

"Someone must remain here that night. It is, as you know, a matter of courtesy that I go. I could ask one of the journeymen to stay in my place, but they are all Tsu's friends and he will wish them to be present. Li might do, but you have a way of handling trouble when it arises, and I would prefer to have you here."

"It is your meaning to leave me in authority?"

"Just that." Tang's eyes twinkled. "Of the entire place and one worthless apprentice, called Fu."

Young Fu made an exaggerated bow. "I appreciate the honor. As for the one of whom you speak, I can manage him with ease."

"I wonder!" was the reply. "Then that is settled. Tell your mother you will sleep here that night."

Small Li was all commiseration. "What ill fortune to

miss this feast! They say there will be no end to the dishes." He smacked his lips at the thought.

When the evening came, Young Fu watched the others swing out of sight, carrying the red packages which would later be presented to the new household. Fu Be Be had worked early and late over a pair of small embroidered wallpieces, and Li was now bearing these as his friend's contribution.

The men had boarded up the store front before leaving, and the youth stood in the small space into which the remaining panel would slide presently and seal the whole. The street was becoming deserted. Pedestrians picked their way in the dusk over loose, slippery flagstones. A load-coolie halted grumbling, leaned his pole with its dangling ropes against his thigh, and counted copper cash. At last, satisfied that his most recent payment had been fair, he tied the coins in his belt, caught up the pole, and went on. The shrill scolding of an old woman rose above the occasional noises of the street as she told her daughter-in-law how to care for the infant son of the household. Young Fu smiled to himself. She reminded him of Fu Be Be. His mother had been proud that Tang had left him in charge tonight, though she had tried to conceal her feeling from him.

The evening sky held no mist. A yellow moon rose from behind the black-blue hills and seemed to come to rest on a summit. The apprentice breathed in Chungking's mixture of odors happily. A food vendor selling roasted sweet potatoes halted before him. "Beggars' food," but good! He threw the man a cash and designated the largest on the trap topping the portable oven. The vendor moved on, and Young Fu tore open the steaming, golden heart. He thought of the delicacies they would have at Tsu's feast. He would not mind being there himself. His head lifted—he would rather be here!

The street was now quite dark and the glow from the moon had not yet touched it. Three men huddled against a doorpost several buildings away. Without curiosity he glanced at them, turned once more to the moon on the summit, then catching at the narrow wooden panel, pulled it along its groove until the street was no longer visible from within.

Securely closed in, he looked about for something to do. A handsome jar lay with oil and polishing cloth beside it and he was soon engrossed with bringing its design into relief. Some day it would be his pleasure to make brasses like this one in his hand. He had an idea for a tiny brazier. Perhaps, if he asked Tang for permission, it might be done after working hours.

The dingy shop, its darkness pricked by the flickering candlelight, glowed with the wealth of burnished copper and brass. Young Fu laid down the jar and roamed about examining the stock. Each article spoke for the man who had created it as clearly as though his name were written on it. Old Tsu made bold, beautiful designs, but he was not always careful. Lu's were all alike, but painstakingly exact. Small Li had a way all his own of making dragon scales, and another journeyman the habit of chipping edges unevenly. But each piece in itself was good. Tang saw to that before his seal was stamped into the shining surface. This small water pipe, a sample of Tang's own craftsmanship, had a rare delicacy. Tang was an artist; it was a pity his time was spent in managing the business.

Young Fu's fingers itched to get at the brazier. He placed the water pipe gently on the shelf and moved into the back room where the oven was. With tongs he lifted away the dead charcoal and blew the flame into life. In the storeroom he found a small sheet of inferior metal. If Tang scolded about his using this! He would have to run that risk. He caught it between the tongs and held it over the red coals. When it was more flexible—

A strange sound claimed his attention. Rats—of course! But he had thought he heard voices. He laid down the tongs and tiptoed to the front room. Everything was as he had left it. Spirits! How Tang would mock such foolishness!

In the furnace room again, he poised the tongs over the fire—that same sound! This time there was no mistaking it for devils. It was followed by the crack of ripping wood. Someone was breaking in the front. He stood frozen with fear. Then, laying the piece of metal quietly to one side, he stuck the tongs slanting in the coals, and crept through to the room adjoining the store. A narrow break in the plaster revealed three figures and back of them the split panel by which they had gained entrance.

As the first turned, Young Fu recognized Wei, the

former employee. Something about the appearance of the others told him they were not Chungkingese, and with their first words he knew them for Southerners.

Wei pointed to the shelves. "Place everything on the floor. Once there it will be a simple matter to throw them into the alley without. Then when our man of importance returns, he may look long for them. By morning the beggars will have them safely hidden." His lips twisted in a malignant smile.

As though rooted to the spot, Young Fu stood watching the rapidly growing pile of brasses on the floor. And then fury stirred him into action. Wei had picked up the water pipe, recognized it as Tang's handiwork, spat on it, and crushed it into the earthen floor under his heel.

The apprentice looked about him wildly for some means of retaliation. The slanting tongs hissed at white heat in the room at the back. In another moment he had rushed with a yell into the store and brought the tongs down on Wei's head with a crash. Wei crumpled on the pile of brasses and his companions raced toward the broken panel, pulling knives from their belts as they ran. Then, realizing that they had only one half-grown youth to combat, they turned upon him.

For Young Fu there began a game of cat and mice around the brasses and Wei's prostrate body. Whenever one of the men neared him, his arms threw forward their deadly weapon. But he could not continue this forever. His heart was pumping violently and his wrists ached from the heavy iron tongs. If he could only reach one of them for a blow! From Wei came an unexpected gurgling sound. The boy's glance slipped to the body below. And in that second one of the other men tripped him. He fell heavily, the tongs clattering across the floor, and waited for a knife in his back. But no blade found him. Instead, Tang's voice thundered out the question, "What business is this?"

The intruders turned hastily, knives upraised. In the doorway stood Lu and Li. Tang had already caught up a large brazier. He aimed it at one of the men, who went down beneath its impact. The other made a desperate attempt to fight his way past the two assistants who blocked his freedom. In the scuffle Li screeched with pain, but twisted the knife victoriously from his assailant's grasp while Lu held him. Within a few minutes the three figures were bound on the floor.

Tang addressed himself to the one still conscious. "You are of this new political party, is it not so?"

The man nodded sullenly.

"This man, Wei, was my enemy—but what of you?"

"He is one of us; moreover, you are rich."

"Rich?" Tang smiled bitterly. "Nine times these past two years have I been taxed for this business; five bags of silver have I given to the militarists. I work as hard as does any coolie. I pay a large squeeze to the Thieves' Guild, and another to that of the beggars, that their members may let me alone. And now you come to tell me that I am rich and must share what is my own. You are not in rags, I see, and your chair-coolie would thank you for those fine leather shoes. Why not give them to him? 'Only the man who can eat the bitterness of bitterness can become the hero of heroes!' " he finished grimly.

An hour later, soldiers, called from the *ya-men*, had taken the men away with them. All three were conscious and able to walk, though Wei's head was badly cut. Young Fu watched them out of sight, then busied himself in straightening the place. Anger stung him again as he lifted a flattened object from the floor.

"What is it?" asked the coppersmith.

"Your little water pipe." Young Fu brushed the dirt from its surface and wondered whether the dents could be worked out. It might again be beautiful, but not as he had seen it earlier that evening. "It was for this I broke Wei's head," he said with satisfaction.

Tang's eyes warmed. "Some day you will make a better one."

"I wish to make a very small brazier," his apprentice told him eagerly. "I took a sheet of metal and was heat-it"—he halted under Tang's amused expression.

"I wondered why the tongs were so ready for your use. But you and I will have no words over that. Tomorrow you may have time to work on your brazier. Perhaps you will bring fame to my door," he concluded teasingly.

"Why did you return from Tsu's so early?" Young Fu wished to know.

"As we entered the house, your friend, Li, told me he had seen Wei hanging about this street. I thought for a little. Then, after we had paid our respects, I explained to Tsu, asked him to excuse me, and told

Lu of my intentions. He insisted on coming, as did Li. It was well that they did so."

The youth shivered. The enemy's knife had been very close to his back. From Tang he caught an expression of understanding. Silence flowed between them in a bond of feeling. At last the coppersmith broke it.

"Go sleep!" he ordered with a drop of the eyelid. "Too much excitement is not good for the very young."

Young Fu turned to the bed. This excitement was little to what there would be when Fu Be Be heard the tale. He laughed to himself. Tomorrow he would rise early and get at that brazier.

"HE WHO RIDES ON A TIGER CANNOT DISMOUNT"

OVER THE NOON RICE the next day Young Fu spoke to Li. "You are a good friend! Had you not seen Wei and mentioned it to Tang, I might not now be here eating rice and green vegetable. But I am sorry you missed the feast."

"I did not suffer too greatly because of that," his

companion replied. "Recently my mother has been anxious for me to marry. The other day I saw her in conversation with an old woman who acts as middle person in arranging such affairs. Last night I recognized that same old woman among the guests at Tsu's. I lost my appetite for remaining. When Tang and Lu started out, I seized the chance to run after them." He wiped his brow at the memory.

Young Fu tormented, "There is no hope for you. You will never escape their clutches."

"No, I suppose not," came the doleful answer. "My sisters are, one after the other, passing through the gate to their new homes, and my mother thinks a daughter-in-law would be useful in the house; she wishes help in caring for the younger children. That I do not care to marry matters little. I would like, at least, one year of freedom. When I was little, everyone in my household ordered me about. After that I had to obey Tang and the other men. Now at last I am doing a man's work, and while I still heed what the coppersmith demands—there is a difference. Good money do I earn," he paused sheepishly, "though, save for two or three hundred-cash pieces, my father is more familiar with that than am I. And a wife would be only an added difficulty."

"She might be beautiful and bring you a great fortune."

"Certainly! The daughter of a mandarin, no doubt!" Li dropped his momentary tone of banter. "She is more likely to resemble the cross-eyed beggar woman that haunts the Lin River Gate."

Later, Young Fu consoled himself with the knowledge that, as yet, Fu Be Be entertained no such ideas for him. He was determined to advance in his work, and he had no intention of permitting anything to interfere with that ambition. With his friend, conditions differed. Li's father was still the head of that house, and until his death his sons would have to accept his decisions for their lives. If Li Be Be had persuaded her husband that a daughter-in-law was desirable in the home, Small Li stood little chance of evading the issue. Young Fu knew that his own freedom of action was unusual. He wondered what his life might have been like had his father lived—a farmer in the country near Tu-To; surely not an artisan in Chungking.

Tonight it was quite possible that to be a farmer in the country would have its advantages. Chair-Makers' Way, usually quiet with the approach of darkness, moved restlessly under the oppressive blanket of heat that enveloped it. Young Fu stirred uncomfortably on the doorstep, counted the days of physical unpleasantness that had already passed, and wondered how many more there would be before the weather changed. He could not remember a hotter summer. It was worse even than last year, when disease had been rampant. And never had so many orders poured into Tang's.

At the moment, his ambition to become a great craftsman lost its charm. His fingers still burned from the feel of hot brasses and his nostrils stung with the acrid odor. He was weary of all drudgery. Just now he wanted never to see a piece of copper again.

Opposite, in a silk store, an apprentice spilt tea on a new roll of Chengtu crêpe and shrieked with pain over the sharp cuffs that came to him in punishment. Young Fu watched with little interest. Apprentices learned in time to become careful with their masters' goods—a lesson he had acquired long ago. Several doors below, two women quarreled about the disappearance of a pair of pasted shoe soles laid in the afternoon sun to dry. Their argument had already reached the stage of discrediting ancestors. A sick baby wailed; a dog snapped and snarled; and swelling beyond all of the other sounds, the muffled beating of a drum with which a priest exorcised evil spirits came from a house where death perched on the rooftree.

Young Fu rubbed his sweating body with the blue cotton jacket which he had discarded, lifted his bare feet from the steaming flagstones for a cooler position, and felt glad that his mother was away from this oven for tonight, at least. Yesterday she had received word from her nephew in the hills, telling of the grandmother's illness. His wife and all of his family were needed every minute in the fields; he wished to know if his aunt could visit them at this time and care for her sister-in-law. Fu Be Be decided that she could, and made immediate arrangements to go.

At dawn her son had accompanied her to the water's edge, bargained for her passage on a ferry, and watched her start across the river. Before leaving, she had placed in his hand two dollars of her carefully hoarded store. "I expect to be away only a little time, but with illness nothing is certain. If I should have to remain, use part of this to pay Old Dai his rent. Hold tightly to what is left. There will be the small matter of the water-coolie, too; give him his money promptly—he needs it to feed the many mouths in his house! As for you who are always hungry—I wonder sometimes what Tang's food is like that it never satisfies your stomach—buy fruit when you feel you are about to starve. That is best in this hot weather. But waste none of it on sesame-seed candy or on sweetened cakes! Cash pieces are not picked up in the streets."

The two dollars lay heavy in the moneybag at his belt; he was acutely conscious of the unaccustomed weight. Two dollars! Why Fu Be Be had left so much in his care he did not know. It was enough to feed a man for two whole months. Dai's rent and the water-coolie and his own small expenditures would not use more than half of it, even if she stayed several weeks. To have a fifty-cash piece in his belt was unusual for him; now to carry two dollars was wealth beyond imagination. And what seemed even more of a dream was that he was, for the first time in his life, left alone with full responsibility for his home and his own actions.

He yawned wearily. It was much too stuffy to go to Wang Scholar's room. And while his nose was quite used to the odor from the pigpen which lay behind his own quarters, on a night like this, one did not seek it out for pleasure. This door sill was little better. He would, he decided, with no one to worry about him, hunt a more refreshing spot. In a moment he had fastened the door to his room securely, tightened his belt, and, hoping to find coolness, slipped through the dark, winding streets to the Lin River Gate.

He soon came out to a low place on the city wall, and clambered to a seat on the broken stone coping. A cool, misty air rose from the river, and his whole body drank it in. Off in the country slept the tiny village, Dsen Gia Ngai—in the spring a jewel of emerald rice fields set in gold mustard. He recalled his errands on the road that led to it. Only a short time ago he had trod it, and now the Land Gate through which he had passed was no longer there. The motor buses that in the beginning had seemed so strange were these days a familiar sight. Passengers crowded them as they plied to and fro on their journeys. As for beggars, the new government was taking care that the wretched hordes did not annoy travelers. Few remained in the old haunts; Young Fu wondered for a moment where they might have gone. He had noticed none of them in the city. This was queer, indeed! It was as if they had vanished into the air. He looked about him. Stars flashed flaming points in the black sky and, below, the river rushed on its way to join the greater Yangtze.

A strange aching disturbed his mind. His memory under the night's spell was a kaleidoscope of romance from many sources. Sages colored the talk of Wang Scholar; in his mother's chatter dwelt fox-women and devils who changed their forms at will; the professional storytellers brought lovers and great heroes to life anew. This city of which he was a part was rich in history, and he was young. Except for two or three occasions, his life had been dull as any girl's. Glamour had deserted the world, he thought with dissatisfaction. Any excitement would be welcome, but there was none. Only tomorrow with its brasses forever waiting to be welded lay ahead. With a sigh he slipped from his place on the wall and started for home.

Lost in thought, he paid little attention to his steps. He had walked perhaps for a quarter of an hour when he became aware that he was in an unfamiliar locality. He stopped and looked about him in the darkness. The street was strange. Slowly he retraced his way in an effort to find the thoroughfare from which it had been entered. He was rewarded by a break in the black street front. Now sure of himself, he turned the right angle. As he did so, a gruff voice hailed, "Who is it?"

Young Fu turned in surprise to find four men grouped on an earthen floor to his left, their hands engaged with a pile of dominoes. The flickering oil cup that gave them light revealed the interior of a straw-sandal shop. In the doorway hung several clumps of tiny sandals for pigs to wear on miry, slippery surfaces. Four pairs of eyes stared at the youth, as he told them he had lost his way, but now knew where he was.

"Where do you dwell?"

"In Chair-Makers' Way."

A swift glance passed between the men. "That is a long walk from this place," remarked one of them kindly.

"Sit a little," suggested another, "and watch the game."

Young Fu felt flattered. This was an experience, indeed! There had been small opportunity in his life for studying at leisure this game which fascinated him deeply. An occasional peek over the shoulders of players had of necessity satisfied his interest. Fu Be Be was bitter in her denunciation of gambling, and as for Tang —any workman of his who appeared morning after morning red of eye and weary of body soon found himself looking for another establishment in which to ply his craft. In such a moment the coppersmith was fond of quoting, "He who rides on a tiger cannot dismount when he pleases." That these harmless-looking little slabs of bamboo and bone had capacity for much evil, Young Fu knew, but that, he told himself, was due to lack of wisdom on the part of players. And to sit here tonight and watch these strangers would, of course, injure no one.

The men were apparently uninterested in their guest. Engrossed in the plays, they said little. The patter of dice and the click-clack of the small rectangles echoed in the dark silence of the deserted street. Young Fu leaned ever closer. His eyes followed each step avidly. His breath came faster. One of the men was playing stupidly. His mistakes were clear. The youth longed to point them out.

Hours slipped by. He had no idea of the time, but he would not now leave until the game was finished.

Suddenly the stupid one flung down his dice, cursed his
bad fortune, and rose to his feet. His companions affected consternation. The game could not be left this
way with accounts unreckoned. Dismayed, they glanced
about them, then one smiled expectantly in Young Fu's
direction. The youth's heart thudded. The words he had
been holding his breath to hear came, "Young man,
will you honor us by taking this man's dominoes?" He
grasped the dice eagerly and awaited his turn.

In what seemed a few swift moments the game was
ended. Young Fu found himself smothered in compli-
ments about his playing. His head whirled. Someone
reckoned scores. Another with a sad expression informed
the guest that he owed three dollars plus a five-hundred-
cash piece. The youth stared open-mouthed. He was
being asked to stand the other's losses as well as his
own. Resentment rose in him. He shook his head in
refusal. "I cannot pay you," he said.

He watched countenances change swiftly. "Were you
born yesterday that you think men play for no stakes?"
they demanded.

"I have no money. Moreover, that other fellow's
debts are not mine to settle."

"You took his place; that is the law of the game."

Young Fu withstood them stubbornly. "I tell you I
have no money. I am an apprentice. If you will tell
how much I owe for my own mistakes in playing, I will
try to send you that amount."

The players laughed harshly. One moved close and
hissed in the boy's face, "You cannot fool us! Do you

think we wasted time on a babe like you without noticing at the beginning that your belt was heavy? You
will pay us, and now!" His hands tugged viciously at
Young Fu's waist, and in a second had loosened the
moneybag containing Fu Be Be's two dollars.

Her son struggled to regain it as the conspirators'
voices shrilled their indignation. "Ai-ya! So he had no
money. He would have cheated us of what is ours.
Liar! Thief!" Feet assisted him into the street accompanied by the warning never to appear in that district
again. Their victim fled round the corner.

In Chair-Makers' Way he slipped over the sill, opened
his own door, and threw himself on the bed. A metallic
dawn foretold a day like the previous ones, but he no
longer cared. Only a few hours ago he had been unhappy about such unimportant things as weather and
a life that lacked excitement. Now he possessed a real
cause. His heart burned like a hot coal in his breast.
Those devils had called him a babe. That was what he
was; as soon as his mother left his side, he fell into
trouble. What a fool he had been! And worse! He was
no better than a thief, for the money with which Fu
Be Be had trusted him was gone as surely as if it had
never existed.

At length his heavy eyelids drooped only to be pulled
apart by the sound of neighbors stirring about morning
rice. He hurried to the shop.

All day long he worked as if under a spell. Twice a
sharp reprimand from Tang recalled him to his task.
He was deadly tired, but he dreaded the return to his

Feet assisted him into the street . . .

home and Fu Be Be. Her scolding he could stand, but not her loss of faith. He had worked hard to make his mother believe in his judgment and ability, and with this one blow he would destroy it all. And her fear that the dominoes might claim him again would color all of their future. She need not worry; he was, after this experiment, more afraid of the game than she could possibly be.

To his relief, Fu Be Be had not returned. A night of reprieve lay before him. He found fruit in the room, ate it hastily and fell into a troubled sleep.

Two more days passed. One noon a load-coolie sought him at Tang's with a message from Fu Be Be. In the hills, farm work was heavy and she was still needed to help care for her sister-in-law, the grandmother. She would be there, perhaps, two weeks longer. She counseled him to seek the company of Wang Scholar in the evenings and to be careful of the money she had left in his keeping.

Young Fu drew his first free breath. So long as his mother remained away, he would not have to account for the two dollars. The thought of Dai's rent which was due the next day and the little matter of the water-coolie squirmed like maggots in his brain. As for adding to his own food, when Tang's left him unsatisfied, that was the least of his troubles.

The next day brought with it Dai's demands and that of the coolie. The second accepted the delay in payment without undue fussing; the first was not so easily appeased. If the present occupants of this room could not pay promptly, there were others in Chung-king who could. "This is a good room in a fine loca-tion and I am foolish to rent it for so small a sum. It is not to be expected that I risk overdue payment on so poor an investment," Dai announced with finality.

"Only a few days," promised Young Fu, "and you shall receive your money."

But where it was to come from he did not know, unless Fu Be Be should return to settle the account. And if she did—his mind started around the same familiar circle of thinking. These hot nights he was famished for water; he had ordered the coolie to stop delivery of this precious article. Lacking it he could neither brew tea to quench his thirst, nor could he cleanse his grimy, sweating body. Dai's scowling de-mands combined with physical discomfort made him thin. He went about his work mechanically.

One afternoon Tang motioned him to an empty cor-ner of the shop. "You have done poor work for days," he began, "you look sick, and you use water as lavishly as if we had a well in the center of the floor. What is the trouble?"

Young Fu managed a sickly smile. "It is nothing. The heat—"

Tang interrupted, "You are young and strong and can bear heat. Only babies and the very old 'Ascend the Dragon' at this time of the year—not those of your age." He paused as an idea came to him. "Did your mother leave you money for your needs?" he asked. "If not I will lend it to you."

Money! All he need do was to lie and Tang would give it to him. To lie was an easy matter. He had done so many times. But he could not remember that it had ever helped him; usually it had led to further difficulties, and his problem was great enough already. Safety lay in keeping this affair absolutely secret. He would yet devise some way out of his predicament. He replied stolidly, "My mother left money with me. It was sufficient."

Tang was not satisfied. His gaze did not leave the youth who stood with downcast eyes and closed lips before him. Young Fu stirred restlessly. If only he might go back to his work. This scrutiny was hard to endure. Suddenly a new fear stirred in his breast. Suppose Old Dai should come to the shop in his effort to collect the overdue rent! His spine prickled at the idea.

Tang spoke again. His voice assumed a new gentleness. "You are worried. I have eyes to see. Why do you not trust me? I am your friend."

This sympathetic approach was more than Young Fu could stand. He commenced haltingly, then the words rushed from his lips in a torrent. Tang soon knew the whole story.

At the end the coppersmith took some coins from his belt. "These will pay your present debts. If your mother postpones her return, I will give you more. When you become a journeyman, you will pay this back in extra work." He lit his pipe and pulled at it once or twice. "There is much I might say to you. You know that such folly repeated would cheat you of your chance to remain in this establishment. You will, I believe, remember before being so foolish a second time. But your mother will probably help you not to forget." He puffed again at the brass pipe, and the water in the bowl responded with the gurgling sound of bubbles.

Young Fu murmured his gratitude and returned to his unfinished task with a lighter heart than he had known since Fu Be Be's departure. Tang was a good master and the affair would not be mentioned again. Before Fu Be Be returned, he would ask the coppersmith to lend him the balance of the original two dollars. Then he would have nothing to confess. His brows knit. Tang expected Fu Be Be to be told. He had said as much. Young Fu's jaw clenched. Tang should have his money back and many thanks for it, as well, but this business of confessing to his mother was his own affair and he would manage it.

As the days passed, he fell once more into normal living. Another message from his mother told him to expect her soon. But strangely enough he was not happy. At unexpected hours some pricking finger of his brain considered telling Fu Be Be all that had happened. Each time he shrugged the suggestion angrily away. He was sixteen years in age—old enough to keep his troubles to himself. Also, he argued in justification, for his mother to know would increase her worries. Under all circumstances silence was the best policy.

One evening he was surprised to find the door ajar and Fu Be Be within their room. She eyed him hungrily. "You are changed," she told him, "are you well?"

Her son reassured her, and she began to chatter about her sister-in-law's improved condition, the rich crops the farm had yielded, the fine air of the hills. She placed her food on the table and Young Fu, sitting opposite, stretched out his arm for a share of it.

"Your appetite is still good, I notice."

The youth nodded absently. How pleasant it was to have a bit of extra food after he returned at night. When they had eaten, they sat talking of many things. The vacation had done Fu Be Be good. She was not the sharp-tongued critic with whom he was so familiar. Her voice ran on happily. "I spoke to them in the hills concerning you. They wished to know if you had contracted any more debts like that of the foreign watch. I told them that you were far from being stupid—one lesson had been enough to give you wisdom; that you worked hard and that your master showed you special favors. Also, that you were beginning to fill your father's place in the household. How many widows did they know, I asked them, who could trust their sons alone in Chungking for so long a time? As for leaving money in their care," she looked up abruptly, "how much of those two dollars have you still with you?"

Young Fu winced sharply. He had been waiting for this question and had prepared himself to remark glibly that the money had been left for safe keeping at Tang's. But this unusual praise from his mother was the last touch. He had within him something too strong to fight. He would have to tell her, no matter how much he lost face. He might as well do it now.

In relating the story he offered no excuses. "I was a fool. You will never trust me out of your sight again. I deserve anything you wish to say to me. There is only one matter about which you need not worry. I am forever cured of playing with the dominoes. The money, Tang is lending me. Later, I am to repay him with extra work. That you are grieved, I know and I am sorry," he finished lamely and waited for the storm to break.

"Since Tang was helping you, it was not necessary for me to know," Fu Be Be said after a long pause. "Why did you tell me?"

"I do not know. I had to do so." Young Fu's fingers picked at a small rough place on the table surface. Finally, he raised his eyes to his mother's and found the other's wet with tears. Fu Be Be lifted a cuff and wiped the moisture away. She looked long into her son's face. Steadily he returned her gaze.

After a time she spoke, "You have become a man overnight."

Young Fu could not believe his own ears. For his mother to receive the news in this fashion was beyond hope. Perhaps she did not understand fully. His face showed his concern.

Fu Be Be soon dispelled all doubts. She rose and commenced clearing the table. Through a broken place in the rear wall she threw a scrap to Old Dai's pigs. Then discovering a new crack in the bowl in her hand, she began to scold her son for his carelessness. "You should handle nothing less durable than brass or copper!"

For the first time in weeks Young Fu laughed. His mother's frown shifted to a smile. "Your amusement overwhelms me with pleasure. Perhaps you will deign to bestow a new bowl on me," she remarked with exaggerated politeness.

Her son laughed again. "Ten!" he assured her, "of the finest porcelain ware." He rose and stretched his arms. His mind was light with a new sense of freedom. Nothing remained to be hidden. And in the morning he would not have to ask Tang to lend him more money.

Instead, when he entered the coppersmith's workshop, he offered the information, "My mother has returned."

The coppersmith glanced at him from under half-closed lids, "And you wish me to lend you the balance of the money you lost?"

Young Fu lifted his head proudly. "Thank you many times! I do not need it. My mother knows all about the affair."

Tang's gaze did not shift, but a subtle change passed over it. "So! And you did not mind losing face?"

"Naturally!" The youth stirred uncomfortably.

After a brief pause Tang quoted, "Medicines are bitter in the mouth, but they cure sickness."

He walked toward the store, and Young Fu, aware of having gained the older man's approval, turned with fresh interest to his work.

"IN THE COURSE OF TIME MEN'S MOTIVES MAY BE SEEN"

THREE YEARS to a day from that misty autumn morning when he and Fu Be Be had first entered the coppersmith's establishment, Young Fu ended his apprenticeship. At the rising hour, his mother went to the chimney, pulled at the loose brick, and took out several five-hundred-cash pieces from her store of savings.

"Take this with you," she told him. "We cannot afford a feast for your associates, but you can use this to buy dessert for the noon meal."

Her son tied the money in his belt and raced off to the shop. To his surprise no one but himself seemed aware of the importance of this date. As the morning wore on and neither Tang nor the workmen made any reference to the occasion, the youth was seized with apprehension. Soon it would be too late to run on the street and purchase delicacies for midday rice. It might be—fear chilled him—that Tang considered his record as apprentice too poor for the advance to journeyman. Anxiously his eyes followed every move the coppersmith made. At last the master, struggling to control amusement, approached.

"You seem hot-hearted about something; are you again in trouble?"

Young Fu could stand no more. "Today—" he began, then hesitated in embarrassment.

Tang waited patiently. "Today?" he repeated questioningly.

"Today—I thought—"

"I understand. You wished to remind me that Wen Mandarin is to receive his order of brasses not later than the Hour of the Monkey. Or is it the commission from the *ya-men* over which you are concerned? We have until nightfall for that delivery. As an apprentice one good trait you have—a fair memory. Were it not for that to your credit—" this time it was Tang's sentence that hung suspended. Suddenly the speaker exploded with laughter. "Tsu," he called as a lull occurred in the anvil room, "we have today another apprentice who thinks he is capable of filling your place. What am I to do about the matter?"

Old Tsu blinked. "Give him the position, of course. For the good of the business I am willing to make any sacrifice. Do you wish me to arrange with the guild immediately?"

Lu interrupted, "Why did you not let me complete this order for the *ya-men* before breaking that evil news? The thought of molding another apprentice into an artisan makes my eye dim and my hand unsteady."

Young Fu stood where he was as the men joined in the laughter at his expense. He could stand their tormenting, now that he knew Tang had not forgotten. He caught at a break in the banter to whisper to the master, "The hour to eat comes quickly. May I use a few minutes to do an errand on the street?"

Permission granted, he hurried to the nearest food shop, made his purchases after careful consideration, carried them back to the place, and told the apprentice in charge of food to serve them with the meal. When the table was laid, a chorus of exclamations arose. Old Tsu squinted at Tang. "Does the new official share his bribes with you that we profit to this extent?"

"It may be that Lu has inherited a fortune and is feasting us!"

Each journeyman in turn disclaimed any knowledge of the bounty. Finally Young Fu rose to the occasion. "My mother and I wish you to accept this very small and worthless gift as proof of our appreciation and good wishes." He bowed to everyone present, sat down, selected choice bits for each man personally, and placed them on the individual bowls.

Before closing time Tang called to him. "You know, of course, that you are to remain here. Your wages will be three dollars for each moon of work. You will eat midday rice here; the other food your house will provide."

Young Fu could not control his surprise. He had expected two dollars a month, and had hoped for a little more. The guild had a sliding scale of wages, and Tang was paying him the maximum for a beginner.

"There have been times," the other continued, "when you have served me better than is to be expected of an apprentice. I do not forget. In the future, any increase in your earnings will depend on yourself."

Young Fu tried to express his gratitude, but the other brushed it aside. "From this time forward you will spend your time welding and designing. Conduct yourself as an artisan should. To be a good craftsman is an honorable estate."

Before they moved apart, Young Fu made a request. "There is one task I wish I might do. I have noticed many times lately the manner in which the silversmiths and jewelers display their wares. Our brasses might be arranged on our shelves to better advantage."

"There is no limit to your own valuation of your ability! And is the accountant likely to esteem your presence in the store?"

Young Fu grinned. "Not if he knows I wish to be there. But there are ways and ways of accomplishing one's purpose. After Wei and his friends were here, the clerk had me help him replace articles in their proper positions. He does not find too much pleasure in such work." It was common knowledge around the shop that the clerk was lazy.

"You may try. If I lose sales in the future, I shall know whose fault it is."

At his first leisure moment the next day, Young Fu walked slowly into the store. His face wore a deep frown. "Tang says these shelves are to be cleaned and put in order, and that I am to help you do it," he grumbled.

The accountant glanced up suspiciously, then, as the other reached for a dust cloth, his expression deepened into satisfaction. "Ai-Ya! but this is a fine way to initiate an artisan. I thought you were Tang's favorite." He hesitated for a moment trying to solve the mystery, then as Young Fu's face continued in its scowl, he continued, "Time it is for me to have some assistance in the work of this place. This new apprentice aids only when customers are in the store; every other minute he is expected to tend furnace. Since Den left, I have had twice as much to do."

Young Fu was lost in contemplation of the shelves. Some of the most beautiful of the smaller objects were hidden completely by the larger ones.

"When will Tang fill your place among the apprentices?" prodded the clerk.

Young Fu admitted, honestly enough, that he did not know. His hands were busy moving things about. That tray as a background for this slender vase, and that handsome brazier in a place by itself—he could not wait to realize his effects. But he must smother his enthusiasm; only in this way would he be able to keep this task as his own.

Soon after this Den entered the store, and Young Fu deciding that enough time had been used on this particular work for one day, returned to his anvil. Moons had passed since Den's departure from the place, but his presence still continued to darken it. He seemed to have any number of excuses for speaking to the accountant. Young Fu wondered at so much leisure. Certainly Wu's business was not prospering if this was evidence of the time his employees had to waste.

Several weeks later Young Fu lifted the jar on which he had been working, hunted for the polishing oil, and sat down to rub the design on the surface into relief. The palms of his hands made a warm friction, and the jar began to glow. He was proud of this piece; he had done every smallest detail by himself. Shape and design, welding and cutting were alike the fruit of his brain and hands, and as he looked at it, he experienced a thrill he had never known before. He raised it on a level with his head, but not for long.

Old Tsu called out, "This is a matter of great importance. We have found one of the treasures from a

Ming Emperor's tomb! Why was I not told of its presence here? A rare work of art, indeed!"

The workmen looked up and Young Fu laughed at his own discomfiture. "I would have judged," he answered impudently, "that it more closely resembled a choice piece of the Han Dynasty. It is too fine to be so recent."

"Every artist thinks himself a genius, until he offers his work for sale," commented Tang wryly.

Den came into the store in time to catch the drift of the conversation. He lounged over the counter and twisted a lip, "So the learned student now thinks himself an artist? Before the moon changes, he will, no doubt, open a shop in the great, new foreign building."

"Who knows?" Young Fu swung about. "Who knows? It may be your betters will yet come to buy from me." He did not mind the badinage of his associates, but Den's remarks were always barbed with poison.

Den gestured largely, "The country fool thinks gold is made of a lump of earth and brass filings."

"The city fool spends his time seeking gain without labor!"

"And has your evil speaking to do with me?" demanded Den.

"As you wish! As you wish!"

A moment of tension was followed by Lu's sharp voice. "Has everyone in this place forgotten the orders to be delivered before the day ends?"

Den made his way to the street. Hot with anger, Young Fu continued to polish the jar. There were moments when the feeling for Den choked him. Never from the first meeting had they felt one spark of friendship. It was small comfort to know that Den was disliked generally, and that even Li who bore no quarrel with anyone, had found the other a difficult companion. His own feeling was something stronger than dislike. With each brief contact anger engulfed him, and later left him feeling beaten and bruised.

It was so tonight. Not until he reached Chair-Makers' Way was he able to erase the memory of the afternoon's altercation from his mind. In Wang Scholar's room he was still distracted. After he had drawn three strokes out of order, the teacher chided, "Thy mind is like a caged animal tonight; to study is useless."

Young Fu put down the pen. He sat silently shuffling the leaves of the book before him, then in a flood of hot words he told of his relations with the offending Den.

Wang Scholar mused. " 'No man is entirely devoid of goodness, and the princely man is tolerant of other men's weaknesses.' "

The youth colored under the reproof. "Tang and the journeymen like him no better," he added in justification.

"Then their tempers are not so easily fired as is thine, for thou hast said that thou and this young man chew the most bitterness."

In the days that followed, Den did not appear so often, but Young Fu gave the fact little thought. He had something else to worry about, and as yet he was ignorant of its nature. An atmosphere of strain held the brass shop in its grip. Tang went about with brows knit

205

tightly together. Old Tsu's sharp eyes darted restlessly here and there as if in search for something he never found. The tall Lu spent much of his time in the store.

Late one afternoon as Young Fu arranged several new samples on the shelves, he was conscious of a stare. Turning in its direction, he found Lu scrutinizing him oddly. "What is it?" he asked impulsively.

The question seemed to pass over Lu's head, for he made no reply. Instead, he stood motionless for another moment, then left the room. With difficulty Young Fu shook off a feeling of depression.

The next day Li snatched at a moment when they were alone to whisper to his friend: "I have discovered the trouble. This morning when I arrived, Tang and Old Tsu were deep in conversation. They did not see me and I, for my part, paid no attention to what they were saying until I heard something about 'dirty fingers.' The theft has to do with the stock on the shelves. Two pieces —what, I do not know—are missing. Tang wished to sell them five days since to a customer, and neither he nor the accountant could find them. Old Tsu and Lu were told, and no one else. Each of these says that he saw the missing articles not more than half a moon ago. All of this I gathered from a few sentences. No robber could have broken into the store. In that case more would have been taken. But if not a robber, then who within these walls would commit such a theft? These new apprentices sleep here and they have no opportunity of handling anything but orders. Everyone else has been here for years." Li scratched his head in a puzzled way and returned to his anvil.

Young Fu felt a wave of sickness. Li's question had been innocent enough, but Li, honest to the core, was not likely to be suspicious, nor was he apt to see immediately that the whole affair reflected on his friend. Four others knew of the theft. Not one of these solved life in such simple terms as did Li. One of them, at least, knew that he, Young Fu, had asked permission to care for the goods on the shelves. Even if Tang had not divulged this fact, two of the others in the secret were aware of the unusual assistance an artisan was giving the clerk. As for the clerk himself he would lose no time in throwing responsibility on the new helper. The very fact that five days had elapsed since the articles were first missed, and that no one had mentioned the affair to him, was conclusive evidence to Young Fu of the trend of thought.

During the day it was this memory that stung him most sharply. The clerk and he had never had much in common, but Old Tsu and Lu had always seemed friendly enough. Tang—he thought of the coppersmith with a pang—Tang and he had been drawn strangely close on more than one occasion. In this effort to value his relationships, it came to him that Tang was the most important figure in his life. Fu Be Be, of course, had first place, but she was, after all, only a woman. Wang Scholar he respected and admired. For Li he felt a protective fondness; in many ways Li seemed much younger than himself. But with Tang there was a depth and warmth to his affection that he gave no one else. If only the coppersmith had come to him directly and spoken of the loss!

Walking home with Li that night, he had little to say. The other's talk ran on the subject of robbers. "There is no proof that ban-keh did not perform the deed. Daily they become of greater strength and power in the province. Men say that never in the history of this land have there been so many. When law-abiding citizens have food and livelihood taken from them by looting armies, the only course left to them is to join the outlaws. And they do not follow the habit of devoting themselves to country districts. Since the Land Gate was torn down and anyone who wishes may go in and out, there is not an alley in this city that lacks their representatives."

Young Fu, dragged from his own unhappy thoughts, replied with a touch of impatience, "Li, do you really think a group of ban-keh would trouble to enter the shop and be satisfied with two pieces of brass?"

"Of course not! I am not so great a fool as that. But in these days of disorder, each man works for himself."

"Perhaps!"

He thought, after they had separated at a junction of the streets, that no matter how greatly he might wish to accept Li's theory about ban-keh, it continued to be improbable. Tang and the others did not consider the idea of robbers from outside. With them the thief was to be found within the walls of the establishment. Then, too, there had been no disturbance to give rise to this thought. The store was never under any circumstances left entirely empty, and a customer with evil intentions would find it no easy matter to accomplish his desires. What was more logical than for Tang to read into Young Fu's request for permission to arrange the shelves, the wish for easy access to the stock? His brain swam. To be thought a thief! This was bitterness such as he had not experienced. Foolish he had been many times, and for it he had carried a heavy heart. But this affair was different. His hands were as clean as those of the master himself. And until some mention of the theft was made, he could not even protest his innocence.

One day followed another with no lightening of the tension. Every person in the place was aware of the undercurrent of trouble. At midday rice, talk was desultory. Tsu's smart quips were few in number. Tang was forever lost in his own thoughts. Young Fu, suspicious of every word or look, fancied that Lu singled him out for harshness; the accountant made sly insinuations that caused the youth to burn with indignation. Once he overheard Tsu ask Lu, "Have you considered Li?"

Lu dismissed the thought as foolish in the extreme. "That one is too honest for his own good."

They moved away and Young Fu consoled himself bitterly with the thought that they were not likely to use the same doubtful compliment concerning himself. Daily he was becoming more wretched. His face grew haggard from sleeplessness. Fu Be Be and Wang Scholar each in turn asked if he were well. He hastened to reassure them. If only Tang would trust him sufficiently to broach the subject of the loss!

But it was he, not Tang, who eventually broke the silence. One evening there was a slacking of work in the shop, and Young Fu left earlier than usual. On the street his feet unconsciously departed from the beaten track, and his eye, caught by a display of brasses, looked up to recognize Wu's establishment. He had passed this way on a number of occasions and had not thought very highly of the wares offered for sale. A figure bent over books on the counter. In the dusk he could not distinguish its identity. Den, probably! He wished no contact with Den, of all people, today. His mind was in great enough turmoil. He would slip away before the other raised his eyes.

As he took a step forward, his glance was held by an object on the middle shelf, close to the door post. Where had he seen that vase before, if not in his own shop? It sat next to the red copper teakettle. Did it? What was wrong with his memory? Only the other day he had placed a jar beside that teakettle; the vase had not been there. Then where had it gone? Certainly not to another brass worker. This was beyond him. Young Fu was galvanized into action. He started to run.

After a few yards of this, he slowed down. He must remember the dignity due his position as artisan. He was not on the way home; nothing would satisfy him now until he settled the question of where that vase had

Where had he seen that vase before?

gone. He would ask Tang immediately if it had been purchased.

He reentered the shop, to find Li preparing to leave. "Ai! Did you think tomorrow had come, that you return at this hour?" Li asked.

His friend caught at his hand in passing, but made no reply. He walked over to the shelves, and Li calling out, "See you again!" passed into the street.

Young Fu searched the stock. The jar and its neighbor, the red copper teakettle, gleamed in the arrangement that his own hands had made. Eagerly his eyes sought the vase. It was nowhere to be seen. Then it must have been sold. But how did Wu happen to have a duplicate? He turned to find Tang and the clerk standing beside him. The accountant's face drew into a smirk. Tang spoke coldly, "What is it you wish? And why do you return at this hour?"

The tone, more than the words, overwhelmed the youth with confusion. "I wished—I wished to locate a—" he stopped abruptly as Tang flashed him a warning glance.

The clerk interrupted, "You see for yourself? It is as I said."

Tang acquiesced. "I will take care of this matter." He turned to Young Fu sternly. "Come with me!"

In a daze the youth followed. When they had reached the furnace room, Tang led him to a secluded corner, then with a swift change of expression, spoke in a low voice, "For what were you searching?"

The story was related. "Was the vase sold?" Young Fu wished to know.

"Perhaps! Promise me you will say nothing to anyone about this until I grant permission. Now go home!"

As the boy passed through the store, he was surprised to see Den leaning on the counter absorbing some tale the clerk poured into his ear. Young Fu gave them a cool glance, then exclaimed loudly. There half-hidden between two larger ones on the shelf stood the vase for which he had been searching.

Tang entered, "Now what is the trouble?"

Young Fu pointed with his chin and reached out. "Here is the vase. It was not in that position when I looked a little while ago, for I moved those two now beside it."

The accountant forced a cool smile. "The country-man dreams. That vase has occupied that spot for several days." He addressed himself to Tang. "The day you wished to show it to a customer and we could not find it, I was sure it would later appear. Afterwards I discovered it hiding in a large jar, mislaid probably by the countryman in one of his moments of playing with the stock."

"And the missing tray—was that also in the jar?" inquired Tang.

The clerk blanched. Before he could speak again, Tang had called Lu from the adjoining room. Den made a move toward the door. A sharp command, "Wait!" halted his steps.

Tang took the vase from Young Fu and held it out to Lu. "Was this article on these shelves today?"

Lu caught at it eagerly. "Of course not!"

"Or yesterday? Or the day before that? Or any time since the hour we first missed it?"

Lu shook his head positively, "Never!"

Tang continued fiercely: "Today Young Fu saw this vase on Wu's shelves. He remembered it, and hurried back to see if that could be the same as this. The vase was gone. Ten minutes later he finds this on the shelf. That Den should have arrived in the meanwhile seems strange, indeed!"

"Did the tray accompany it?" asked Lu.

"The tray I suppose still sits in Wu's store. I cannot credit Wu with so little brain as to think he knows about them. I shall leave that to the guild to learn."

At the word, guild, Den looked up sullenly. "Wu though not so remarkable an artisan as you, Honorable Coppersmith, has wits of his own. He regretted that I knew so little about brass work, and to save my face, I told him I would make some designs that he lacked. I borrowed this vase and tray and copied them in odd moments. Wu thinks they are his own product. He liked the vase so well that he placed it for display in a prominent position. I did not dare to move it, though I knew the risk I ran should someone from this place come that way." Den's voice was now shrill with bitterness. "As my ill fortune would have it, it was the countryman." He turned from Tang to Young Fu. "From our first meeting your hands have emptied evil on my head. My

214

family, for months, chided me for not winning your apprenticeship for my cousin. From the beginning Tang took your part against me. Old Tsu and the journeymen followed like sheep. They grudged me a civil word. Fortune ran on your heels. You studied with a teacher; you gained trade from the foreign woman; you saved Tang money on the Hochow trip. It was Young Fu this and Young Fu go here and Young Fu do that! Always Young Fu, until I was sick of the name. When Wu invited me, I determined to make a fresh start. I would have done anything to please him, and I have not been unsuccessful." His voice broke suddenly.

"And what has this to do with you?" Tang asked the clerk.

"Nothing!" interrupted Den hotly, as he stepped between them. "The fault is all mine and I will bear the penalty."

"Hush!" Tang pushed Den aside. "Why do you hide behind this youth?" he demanded of the accountant. "If you had nothing to do with this affair, then why did you lie just now about the vase, and why try to cast suspicion on Young Fu?"

"Because I believed the countryman guilty. Also, I wished to help Den."

" 'Disease enters by way of the mouth; most of men's troubles come out of it.' True, Young Fu handled the stock; did he also have freedom with the money box? If not, why do not some of the accounts agree with the silver in hand?" The clerk's eyes were wide with terror, as Tang continued, "This idea of the brasses was not

Den's. How much money did you get for lending them to him?"

Den was speechless. After a time the clerk gained sufficient control of his voice to reply hoarsely, "Den said that Wu wished him to design something of his own. It was one of Wu's reasons for offering him the position; he thought Den might have some original ideas."

Lu snorted, "Original! Den was all right with accounts, but he hardly knew one brass from the other."

The accountant seized at the interruption, "I knew that; I wished to help him; always I liked Den more than I did the other apprentices."

"And you did this service for nothing?" Tang pressed the question.

"He was to pay me a little from his wages each month. I needed money."

"So it would seem!"

Tang turned again to Den. His tone became milder. "You have risked much for this fellow."

"He was the only one in this place that ever showed me kindness," was the retort.

"That I regret. You have a way about you that repels men. But some good qualities you have. For that reason you will go unpunished. I do not believe you are naturally without honor. Perhaps intimacy with this man has been bad for you." Tang sighed wearily. "As for the tray, bring it here so that we may turn it and the vase into something else. Wu may keep the design you stole; I will make new ones."

Den thanked him and was gone.

"What is to be done with you, I do not know," Tang turned again to the accountant. "For five years I have trusted you. When I learned recently that you were gambling," the clerk could not conceal a start, "I began to watch you. It was not long before your accounts refused to balance. Then when the two brasses disappeared, I knew you had something to do with their loss. I could send you to the *ya-men* for punishment, but I prefer to handle my own problems. You will remain to reckon accounts, though in the future I shall check carefully what is received. You will not play with the dominoes again!"

"If I refuse?"

"There is always the *ya-men*."

The journeymen who had crowded in the adjoining room now filed through quietly on the way home.

That night Young Fu repeated the story to Wang Scholar.

"Did I not say," remarked the teacher, "that no man is entirely devoid of goodness? Thy enemy, Den, possessed a rare loyalty for his friend."

"And I did not realize before how bitter a part I played in his life."

" 'In the course of time, men's motives may be seen.' Jealousy is a strong passion for a youth to conquer!" the older man said gravely.

The next morning there was no sign of the accountant. At noon another man filled his place.

"I did not expect him to stay," offered Lu. "In this shop he could never have been without shame."

"That was why I gave him the opportunity to run away. I wish no expensive court cases at this time. There are too many other uses for my money. He is heavily in debt, and, had he remained, we might have suffered greater losses than we did. As it is, we are rid of him," was Tang's reply.

Young Fu looked up cheerfully. The cloud had lifted and he felt like a new creature.

"Have you inherited a fortune?" asked the coppersmith in passing.

The other beat a dent with his hammer. "This is a different place in which to work," he suggested. "I thought that you and the others suspected me of the theft."

"That our actions wore that appearance, I admit. It was for a purpose, as you know. So long as the guilty man thought the blame rested on you, he made no further move. I wanted to discover what had happened to the brasses before taking action."

Young Fu lowered his voice, as quiet reigned suddenly in the room. "I could not understand when you did not ask me about the loss."

"You were not supposed to know of it."

"No, but that did not make the trouble easier to bear. I could endure the distrust of the other men, but not yours."

Tang gave him a long look. "Until last night, I alone knew for certain that the clerk was guilty. I took Lu and Tsu into my confidence about the lost brasses and asked them to help me solve the mystery concerning them. Both men were favorable to you, but they knew you had an equal chance with the clerk of stealing, and more opportunity than anyone else in the shop. That fact created suspicion in their breasts. Does it make you happier to know that I told them I trusted you as I would my son, were he here?"

Young Fu could make no reply, but the coppersmith seemed satisfied as he walked on. Tang trusted him as his son, he repeated over and over in his mind. If he were younger, he would recognize this moisture under his eyelids as emotion; since it was not that, it must be smoke that had drifted to him from the furnace. He raised his hammer in the air and pounded violently on the sheet of metal beneath.

A
USE
FOR
CURIOSITY

WITHIN THE YEAR, Li was married. Li Be Be finally arranged a suitable match for him with the daughter of an old acquaintance, a maker of fans. For days her son's round, pleasant face wore a disconsolate expression, but later he decided to accept his fate calmly. "There is no help for it!" he confided to Young Fu.

"Have you ever seen the girl?"

"Once when she was about six years old her parents brought her to our home at the time of Lantern Festival. I was three years older and, of course, paid no attention to a girl. What she is like, I have no idea." Li sighed. "I hope she has a good disposition. If not, my mother—" he left the completion of the sentence to his hearer's imagination. "This will be the first outside woman to live under our rooftree," he concluded.

His friend comforted him. "I understand. You are a good fellow, Li, and deserve the best wife in Chung-king."

That night Fu Be Be was told of the impending feast. "I wish," her son informed her, "to go to the *t'sai-feng* whose tailoring shop is two doors from the end of this street, and order a garment."

"Will you be so good as to tell me who is paying for this?"

"Certainly! I am."

"Perhaps you have wealth that I know not of. In that case you will doubtless send some of the handsome Tibetan tapestry for your gift, and will later entertain the couple at the new foreign eating place on the main street, where it is said that only foreign food is served, and the guests have no more breeding than to stab and carve their food with steel instruments."

"That, too, I should like to do sometime, if for no reason save to find out what foreign food is like." His thoughts swung for the moment to the foreign woman. He had not seen her in months. In the last political upheaval, the foreigners had been forced to leave the city, due, most likely, to what their enemies had rumored about them. Few of the southern agitators were now in Chungking, but their doctrines were still prevalent.

"You have strange tastes," continued Fu Be Be. "I think too much of my stomach to partake of such dishes. As for this matter of the tailor, I shall buy the material and make your clothing, as usual."

Her son rejected the proposition stubbornly. "I waste no money in other ways. A good garment at this time I consider important. Even if it mean sacrificing in some other way, I wish it. The clothes that you make for me are sewed more neatly than are any in this city, but their fashion is still that of the farm lands. Since the first day we came here, I have been aware of that, but there was nothing I could do about it. We had no money. That even now we have to count each cash carefully, I know also. It does not change my determination about this garment. Some day I intend to be an important man in my guild. The earlier they forget that I am a country-man, and that this city is not my native place, that much sooner shall I be on the path to fortune."

Fu Be Be raised no more objections. Her son was a man, earning a journeyman's wages, and it was true that he wasted little. What his ambitions were she did not know, but that he would be successful she believed absolutely. He had a clever head, and for years fortune had favored him. Part of this was due to her constant attentions to Kwan Yin's shrine; so long as she lived, there would be no neglect of these offices.

She spoke again, "When you go to the tailor's shop, I will go with you and watch him cut the material."

"You may go with me to buy the silk, but I go to the *t'sai-feng*'s alone."

"To buy the silk!" Fu Be Be repeated shrilly. "Have you lost your senses? Since when did artisans wear silk?"

"Tang wears silk garments, and Old Tsu has a black satin jacket for dress occasions."

"Tang is a well-to-do merchant, and Tsu, so you have told me, has many sons to bring money into his house!" Fu Be Be's indignation knew no bounds.

"Wait a little! Wait a little!" begged her son. "At Ling's silk shop opposite there is a piece of gray flowered damask with two or three defects in the weaving. I have examined it on two occasions, and, with careful cutting, the flaws may be discarded. Ling will sell it cheaply; he has already quoted a low price for the number of feet I need, but you may go with me to bargain for it."

With the silk purchased, Young Fu sought the tailor. While he waited in the shop for the *t'sai-feng* to finish with another customer, he watched the workmen. One swept the pressing iron, a small pan with a closed lid under which charcoal burned, over a series of seams; another used a narrow steel band, open at both ends, as a thimble to plunge a short needle into corded fasteners. The youth wondered how they could be content to work in such fashion day after day. A hammer and anvil was more to his liking.

The tailor approached with a smile, listened to this new patron's desires, took measurements, and considered the piece of material. "You have, I fear, not quite enough of the silk. If I am extremely careful in the cutting, I may be able to make shift." He frowned over the difficulty presented.

"That you will succeed where another tailor would fail, I feel sure. If you are not too busy, I shall remain here while you cut it."

The t'sai-feng smiled tolerantly, "Tonight I have many affairs. I shall have to wait for leisure to accomplish this matter."

"When will you have such leisure—tomorrow?"

"Perhaps!"

"Then I will take this home with me and return at the same hour tomorrow night." He wondered if this tailor thought he was born recently, that he would leave the cutting of material to the other's honesty.

A shrug of the shoulders and the t'sai-feng capitulated. "Very well! I will put these other important matters aside and cut the garment now."

Young Fu watched the process like a hawk. As each scrap of goods fell away, his fingers collected it. At the end he had several pieces of good size and a number of small ones. These bits of silk would serve Fu Be Be for a dozen purposes."

Li's wedding day came and went. Young Fu clothed himself in the new apparel, and felt a kinship with all who were wealthy. Fu Be Be's eyes could not entirely hide their pride as she exclaimed with simulated horror, "Hurry to your feast! Should the landlord see you, our rent would become double."

Tang raised eyebrows when he saw the youth and asked, "Is it Li's wedding feast or yours?"

Young Fu grinned in reply. Such talk was harmless. He was, at least, in these garments not to be dubbed "the countryman."

At the end of a moon, Li was still elated over the bride's disposition. She was not too bad to look at, and she strove in every way to please his mother. What he had feared most had not come to pass. Peace reigned under his father's roof.

Conditions were as usual in the shop. A new apprentice had joined the group. There were three of them now. Young Fu wondered at Tang's patience with them. Had he ever been so clumsy and stupid? His first year as journeyman closed, and Tang increased his wages a dollar a month. When he announced the good news to Fu Be Be, she was jubilant. "All of this dollar can be saved."

"Most of it," corrected her son. "A part must be used for rent. This room of Dai's has known our presence long enough. Two rooms, even though small, are what we need."

His mother continued to fret about the extra expense, but she did not delay her search for new quarters. She, more than Young Fu, would appreciate this release from the cramped space in which she had spent her Chungking life.

Wang Scholar received the word calmly as he did all else in life. "I shall miss thee and thy mother's thoughtfulness, but thou wilt, I hope, return to me here often. A quick student hast thou been. Let thy mind rest often in the wisdom of the sages; there thou wilt find the true secret of living."

"Too much I owe you for me to forget the debt easily," replied the youth. "The first night I stood on this door sill you were kind to me, a stupid youth new to the ways of this city. Since then you have shown me one goodness after another. Now you attain great age and I am young and strong. If you have need of anything so unworthy as I have to offer, send me word through the Ling household." Long since he had taken Wang Scholar to call on Father and Mother Ling in the pleasant room where Tang had installed them, and intimacy had developed between the two old men.

Fu Be Be was successful in finding two rooms that cost little more than Dai's one, and had no pigpens at the rear. She arranged her possessions proudly. This was not bad after only four years of residence in Chungking. She would plan for an early visit in the hills that she might let them know of her good fortune, and indirectly of her son's ability. Were it not for the dangers attendant on travel, she might count on a brief return to her own village. But even without bandits and soldiers, there was the problem of cost. She was, she told herself, becoming as spendthrift as her son. Some time when his success had been proved, she would go there and select a wife for him. One of these pleasure-loving city maidens was not her idea of what was acceptable for a daughter-in-law. A young woman from the farms, who could prepare good food and care thriftily for a household, was more to her liking. Her son, however, was still young and there was plenty of time in which to decide so important a question.

More and more frequently Tang sent Young Fu on errands that demanded a man's sagacity. He it was who now bargained in the homes of the wealthy and ordered an apprentice about, as he himself had once been commanded. When he was in the shop, most of his moments were spent at Tsu's side designing. For this branch of the work he had talent. Lu remarked ironically that in so far as that fact was true, it was good. Certainly Young Fu would never cause anyone to exclaim over his work in welding!

The object of this comment smiled impudently. "It is not expected that a man be perfect in everything!"

Lu groaned, and Old Tsu quoted with a chuckle, "'The monkey looks in a mirror and wonders at the charm of his own reflection.'"

Tang, his eyebrows drawn together in perplexity, called to the youth in passing, "Come here! I wish a few words with you."

When Young Fu reached him, the coppersmith continued, "I have here a note requesting my presence at the *ya-men* tomorrow morning. The reason for it I know no more than do you. But a *ya-men* does not invite men to drink tea and make polite conversation. Because of that fact, I wish a companion. Tsu is growing old for such worries and Lu is too blunt for official meetings. You will clothe yourself in the garment you wore to Li's wedding and meet me without the *ya-men* gate at the Hour of the Dragon. Naturally, I wish no one to know where we go."

Young Fu was elated. In his new garment he would resemble one of Tang's intimates rather than an employee. Tang had not said so, but then! That silk had been a good investment, indeed.

The following morning he left the house in his usual workman's suit. There was plenty of time before seven o'clock, and he would take advantage of the new public bathhouse before changing to the silk which he had managed to carry from his home without Fu Be Be's knowledge. He entered the building, paid his fee, and, his toilet completed, gave the man in charge an extra cash to hold his soiled clothing until later in the day.

Tang met him promptly and sent in his card to the official clerk. They were soon ushered into a large reception room in which sat men of varying stations in life. Young Fu wondered at the reasons for their presence in this place. As Tang had said, one was not invited to a *ya-men* for pleasure. A load-coolie with bowed head stood with hands still clasping his carrying pole. What business had this toiler here? Memory of another bearer who, for no reason at all, had been deprived of his life flashed through the youth's mind. He shivered slightly. Almost he had succeeded in conquering his aversion to soldiers and those in authority, but not entirely. An oily-looking merchant shifted his eyes nervously from one face to another. A farmer bent under the burden of a heavy wooden yoke that collared his neck. Uniformed

Uniformed guards moved about.

guards moved about. One stood with musket directed
toward two men manacled together. Young Fu felt his
flesh creep. This room sent his spirits to their lowest level.

A clerk approached. "I wish one Tang, a coppersmith."

Tang arose. "That is my unworthy name and trade."

"Please follow me!"

He led them through many corridors and halted
where another attendant stood before a door. "Advise
Dong Official that Tang, the coppersmith, waits."

The attendant entered the room. In a moment he returned. "Dong Official will receive Tang Coppersmith
at once."

Tang followed the attendant and Young Fu waited
restlessly in the hall. So this was simply another order—
Dong Official was the one who had given them a number of past commissions. But he had always sent them
by one of his servants. Tang would be provoked over this
misleading note to appear at the *ya-men* without any
idea of the business involved. It was time wasted. Also
he himself had enjoyed a steaming bath and the pleasant
feel of his best clothing, only to return immediately to
the grime of the shop.

The attendant still braced himself against the door.
Young Fu glanced at him curiously once or twice, then
turned his attention elsewhere. He wondered where all
of these winding ways led. Which doors opened to trial
courts? which to torture chambers? which to dungeons?
What of the men within them? Were they all criminals?
A sinister sadness which one at times sensed dimly in

the Chungking streets centered in this building. Why was Tang so long?

The first sight of the coppersmith's face, on reappearance, proved that this conference with Dong Official had not dealt with an order for work. Young Fu had never seen the older man so worried. They were once more in the street before Tang spoke. What he said took the other's breath away. "Lu is suspected of opium smuggling!"

"Lu! Our Lu?" This was too hard for Young Fu to believe.

Tang nodded gloomily. "The affair is strange indeed. Opium has been found in a small shed at the rear of Lu's house. The place was once used for pigs, but in the last year cast-off articles have been stored there. A few days since, spies from the *ya-men* discovered that opium was being smuggled from that section to a junk on the river, carried down to the city of Ichang and sold, at much less than government charges, to a foreigner from Shanghai. The sweet, penetrating odor of the drug betrayed its presence in Lu's shed."

"But Lu—" began Young Fu.

"I know," Tang interrupted. "I could not credit my own ears while Dong Official spoke. He sent for me today to inquire concerning Lu's reputation and that of his household. The opium has not yet been seized. Spies who are watching the house are using it as bait to catch the smuggler. If in three days more they have caught no one, Lu as head of his house will be imprisoned."

"Lu is no smuggler!"

"Of course not! I told Dong Official I was willing to vouch for Lu himself. He is no more guilty of the crime than you or I. His three sons, all of whom are married and live under his roof, are hard-working artisans. Other than that I do not know."

"Perhaps Lu might know who in his household would be likely to do such a thing."

"Lu is not to be given that chance. Dong Official bound me to secrecy. I told him I had an assistant who might do some spying unsuspected by Lu's family. At first he hesitated, but after a little agreed to let me tell you. I shall find some excuse for sending you to Lu's house today, and you will use your eyes while there."

Young Fu's heart beat faster at this fresh instance of Tang's trust in him. At the shop he went about his work mechanically. The whole matter had a tinge of unreality, as though it had come from a public storyteller's lips. That Lu, blunt and direct in all his ways, could no anything requiring the plotting and secrecy of smuggling was absurd. Moreover, the game was a supremely dangerous one. Opium was worth its weight in gold. If the high government tax could be avoided, its sales brought unimagined returns. If the high government tax could be avoided! That was the reason men sought so many devious ways of getting the drug down the river.

The youth's mind flew back to the farm land near Tu-To. There had been fields of poppies all about them; even on their own small bit of ground a portion had been planted with the delicate, fragile blooms. Splashes

of gorgeous color they had made against the green of
beans and sweet potatoes, but Young Fu could remember that his father had loathed them. For the
poppies were not of the farmer's planting. Each year
the Tuchun saw to it that the farmers gave part of their
land for this purpose. Poppies yielded opium and in no
other way could a man responsible for troops find so
easily the money essential to their maintenance.

It was said that the drug had first come to China
from India, a land to the south. There had been immediate proof of its possibilities for evil. It devoured
the minds and bodies of the men who used it. It ruined
fortune and happiness for family after family. It caused
a war between China and the foreigners. The Chinese
began to whisper the word in dread. No curse like it
had ever touched the Middle Kingdom. And then the
government at Peking had issued an edict against the
growing of poppies and the sale of the drug derived from
them. A merchant caught dealing in it paid with his
life. Farmers found that cultivating even one spray of
red blossom lost them their heads. As if by a miracle,
the curse loosened its clutch about the country's throat.

And then wars had come, and more wars. Generals,
short of funds and with the law in their own hands and
not in those of a central government, forced the farmers
in their districts to plant poppies once more. The color-
ful fields had sprung up overnight, among them those of
Young Fu's memory. And men were again using the
drug commonly. But the local governments still kept an

exorbitant tax on its sale, and smugglers, when caught, paid dearly. The thought of what might happen to Lu caused a prickling of the skin.

All day long Young Fu expected Tang to send him on the errand to Lu's house, but nothing happened until after Lu had left the shop for the night. Then the coppersmith held out a package and gave his directions. "Take this brazier to Lu and ask him if he considered it finished. Tell him that it is to be delivered tonight instead of tomorrow morning. That I have just made this decision is not for Lu to know. He will, of course, extend the courtesy of refreshments and you will make the most of that time. Study those present and when you have found out all that you can, leave. After departure, walk around to the back of Lu's house and see what you can see."

Young Fu left, the brazier clutched in his hand, his pulse quickening with excitement. He found Lu finishing his evening meal, and was invited to share the food. As was the custom, the daughters and daughters-in-law of the household disappeared with the entrance of this eighteen-year-old artisan. Only Lu's settled wife and the men and boys remained. The visitor's eyes roved from one face to the other. He discussed the health of everyone present and of his own absent mother; he agreed that rice was higher than for months, that bandits were increasing, that the present government was an improvement. None of these supplied him with a clue. These were honest, industrious people; it was nonsense to think of them in connection with smuggling.

He remained as long as he could courteously do so. Lu thought the brazier had to be delivered at once and would misunderstand further delay on the part of the guest. When the ceremonies of leave-taking were at an end, Young Fu lost himself in the shadows of the street, then retraced his steps and endeavored to locate the rear of Lu's property.

In the dark the task was doubly difficult, and against the winding walls that protected these buildings it was hard to decide where Lu or his neighbors dwelt. A figure rose suddenly to face him. "Your business here?" it demanded.

Young Fu could hear his own heart thud with fright. He held out the brazier. "My master's chief artisan lives in one of these houses," he controlled his voice sufficiently to say. "This piece of brass I was sent to show him before delivering it to its owner."

The figure examined the brazier, lifted the openwork lid, found it empty and closed it. Then he ran his fingers all over Young Fu's body, gave him a rough push and ordered briefly, "Go!"

Young Fu went. He had reached the shop before breath once more began to come freely. Neither he nor Tang had anticipated a meeting with one of the ya-men spies. He burst out with the tale to the coppersmith's interested ears.

"And you saw nothing that might be questionable in Lu's household?"

"Nothing," Young Fu admitted dismally.

At the end of the three days, Lu to his own horror

and that of his family was marched to the *ya-men*. Tang sent gifts to Dong Official to ease Lu's treatment while there, and asked that trial be postponed as long as possible. With Lu went the supply of opium that had been hidden in the shed.

In his bereft home sorrow reigned. The unexpectedness of the whole proceeding had left its members dazed. Young Fu called that night. He wanted to know if they had any plan for discovering the real criminal.

"Plan?" asked the eldest son. "How can we plan when we did not know until this morning that the opium was there?"

Their guest felt a twinge of irritation, then he realized these men were so thoroughly overwhelmed by the calamity that had befallen them, that it would take time for them to regain their poise. "Would you permit me to look at your shed?" Young Fu wished to know.

In a moment he had passed through the house and entered the shed at the rear. The small building lay close to the main one. It was several feet from the street wall, and anyone coming from outside by climbing that barrier would be visible to both wings of the home. Young Fu decided to experiment. But first, he would thank his hosts and rid himself of their doleful companionship.

Five minutes later he stood without the back wall. Tonight with the opium and suspect safe behind *ya-men* bars, no spy accosted him. What fools they were, he thought, to leave no one on guard. But then, the officials were not so sure of Lu's innocence as he. He wondered what poor Lu was bearing at this hour. Had he been tortured to confess? Under such methods men frequently admitted to crimes with which they had nothing to do. If only he could find some clue to lead to the guilty wretch who had placed the opium in Lu's shed. If Lu's fate depended on his sons, it was already settled. Young Fu was not impressed by the brains of the household. Of course, Lu himself did not compare with Tang or Old Tsu in wits, but he was a good man and a fine artisan.

As for this wall facing him—he had scaled higher ones than this. Stealthily he climbed to the top, then flattened himself along the plastered surface. As his eyes became used to the darkness, he recognized the outlines of the shed and the wall that divided Lu's property from that of his neighbor. The shed leaned against this separating barrier. Why had he not noticed that when he entered the yard with Lu's sons. What was that? Something had moved beyond that wall. Young Fu strained his eyes to no avail. A dog, perhaps! If so, it would soon scent him out on the coping. The sound came again, followed by a fumbling, scratching noise. This, too, might be a dog. Suddenly his nostrils were aware of a cloying odor—he breathed out in distaste. Opium! Someone was handling opium beyond the wall which adjoined the shed!

Unexpected quiet reigned. Young Fu lay hugging his plastered coping. In the street below him a footfall padded swiftly. He slid down and pursued the steps. It required but a few seconds to catch up with the shadowy figure ahead. He had no proof that this man was the one he wanted, but such risk would have to be run. Into one street and another the shadow led him; for a time they climbed, then started abruptly down an incline. Mist from the river rose to meet them. Damp earth was under their feet. The figure halted and looked over his shoulder. Young Fu sank silently behind tall grass. He lay still while the other moved a few paces forward.

A tiny light, probably a small lantern flame, pricked the blackness three successive times. A ricebird called. The light appeared again and the oars splashed the water. Three flashes of a lantern and the call of a ricebird were the signals. Fools! Did they not know this was not the season for ricebirds?

Another figure joined the one on shore. Their whispers drifted to Young Fu's ears. The steward on the foreign steamer would place the packet in a foreign valise, in an American passenger's stateroom. The valise would be hidden under the lower berth, and removed after the passenger had left the room at Ichang. In a foreigner's room the contents of the packet would be safe; on this boat only Chinese passengers were searched for opium. The conspirators laughed—it was this very steward who helped the customs' officers hunt for concealed opium.

Young Fu's mouth closed grimly. Perhaps tomorrow they would not laugh! And Lu had been imprisoned for what was taking place here on this river bank.

A little later the youth found himself once more tracking a shadow through the Chungking streets. The man, as Young Fu had expected, did not return to the house next to Lu's. Instead, he halted several doors below. To remember the house would be simple, but otherwise there was as yet no way of identifying the smuggler. The two voices had revealed no distinguishing features; they had come to him in whispers. He wondered if he could force the man to speak. Then an idea came to him. Emerging from the doorway in which he had been hiding, Young Fu staggered up the middle of the thoroughfare and sobbed, as he neared the man waiting for admittance, "My father's money! My father's money!"

Surprised, the other turned abruptly. "Take your troubles from this neighborhood," he warned.

Young Fu softened his cries. "If I had never touched the dominoes, my father would still have his money."

"Who cares what your father has? Leave this street before I summon a *ya-men* runner!"

Young Fu left. He would not soon forget that voice. It was raucous as a magpie's. He continued to sob until he turned the corner, then sped to Tang's.

Early the next morning, Dong Official was told the story. The man with the magpie voice was arrested and, under torture, betrayed the names of his accomplices. Their method had been to conceal the drug in unlikely places, and collect it again when opportunity offered. Lu's rubbish shed had been ideal for storing the drug between the trips of the foreign steamer. It had been reached from the next yard by the simple process of digging under the wall against which the building leaned. The tenants of this property, Lu's neighbors,

239 |

were an aged couple who suspected nothing. For months opium had been hidden in small quantities under loose flagstones in their yard. The prisoner had been in the act of collecting one of these supplies when Young Fu had first discovered him. The band had learned of Lu's arrest and had realized the danger of lurking spies in that section. But they had feared the loss of this hidden store, too, and the man in custody had offered, for an extra sum, to run the risk. And then he had been caught by this callow youth! That was almost as bitter to taste as torture.

Through Don Official's intercession, Lu was released speedily. He had been imprisoned only a day and a night, but he looked ten years older. His steps were those of a sick, old man. Young Fu, walking through the *ya-men* courtyard with Lu and Tang, lowered his eyes to hide the pity in them. Tang, when they were once more in the bosom of Lu's speechless family, suggested that his chief artisan rest for a few days. Perhaps a little visit in the country would be a good plan. Lu accepted this thoughtfulness with a murmur of politeness, but his expression of misery did not change. The youth wondered what had happened at the *ya-men*. That, it seemed, was a matter on which Lu's lips would not open readily.

Young Fu's attention was diverted by the interest and admiration the family was centering upon himself. Their gratitude was overwhelming. He was glad when Tang suggested a return to the shop. Even a year ago, he told himself, he would have delighted in their commendation. That he no longer did so was evidence of development. He deserved no special praise for what he had been able to do for Lu. His motive had been to serve Tang, for whom he would attempt most things. The gods had given him a quick eye and ear, and good fortune had prompted him to scale the wall at that time. Nothing else had been required but to follow the figure he suspected.

Life's ways were strange. He, for no apparent reason, had one stroke of luck after the other. Lu, an innocent, hard-working soul, had been caught by ill fortune in a net of worry and disgrace. Fu Be Be would warn him against such thinking. It was not wise to consider the ways of the gods with men. He walked into the shop behind Tang and in a short time was lost in a new design for a vase.

"ONE MUST FIRST SCALE THE MOUNTAIN IN ORDER TO VIEW THE PLAIN"

Lu did not return at the end of a few days. Weeks passed before he acquired strength and courage to take up once more the normal tasks of living. In his absence the journeymen shared in his labors.

Young Fu was confined for longer hours to the anvil and furnace room. This was the branch of the work he liked least. To design a new pattern answered some deep-seated need of his being; to do important errands and bargin with customers exercised his wits. This business of welding and cutting was work any artisan could do, he justified himself, even while he admitted the truth of Lu's former remarks concerning his inaptitude for these lines. Here was where his friend, Li, shone. Li's seams were always beautifully joined, and he enjoyed making them so. Tang said Li was developing into the kind of journeyman any brass shop might desire.

"This experience is excellent for your training," Tang told Young Fu one morning during Lu's continued absence. "We shall make a good workman of you yet. You are beginning to mold kettles less like those a water buffalo might be expected to turn out." The listeners laughed, but Young Fu, sweating over the work he loathed, did not smile. For the rest of the forenoon his face held to its sullen expression. Old Tsu ventured an ironical remark and received a scowl in return.

Later in the day Tang called the youth aside, "You disappoint me," he began flatly. "You have, I fear, been spoiled by too much good fortune. This is, after all, a brass shop—not a place to rear the pampered sons of the wealthy. Each part of the work is as important as another. Were it not for men who turn naturally to the furnace and anvil, we should have no need for the store, or," he paused for emphasis, "for designers!"

Young Fu winced under Tang's level gaze. Without a word in reply he turned and resumed his work. He was hot with fury. He worked hard—he was not a pampered

son of the wealthy, nor had he been spoiled by too
much good fortune! He caught up his hammer. How
he would like to beat the jar on which he was working
out of recognition! His hands were shaking. With
difficulty he steadied himself. As he labored, he took a
new interest in the article. He would let Tang see that
he could make as good seams as any man in this place.
He would let Tang see! During the hours that remained,
he took painstaking care with the jar. He would leave
this anvil for nothing, if he could avoid it. Fragments
of Tang's speech recurred constantly. Disappointed in
him! That was unfortunate, but Tang could recover without his assistance. This coppersmith was not the only
man in the Middle Kingdom, or, for that matter, in
Chungking! Then why, his mind asked him, did he
let the other's words annoy him so greatly? He shook
the thought from him.

Tang gave him a cool nod as Young Fu said, "Good-
night!" Sore of heart the youth passed into the street.
At home he was restless. If he were still at Dai's, his
feet would inevitably have sought Wang Scholar. Perhaps it was better that Wang Scholar was not so close.
This was a matter that concerned him and the
coppersmith alone. Bed was no comfort. He rose
earlier than usual and hurried to the shop. Within
him was no desire to meet Tang, but the place drew
him like a magnet.

A new piece lay before him. On it he concentrated
all of his attention. When he had finished with it, he
was conscious of satisfaction. He defied anyone to say

this was not good workmanship. He looked long at the object and realized wearily that he cared little what anyone thought about it. Only one thing mattered— Tang was disappointed in him. And rightly so! Instead of trying to do this part of the work well, he had shirked whenever possible. For a youth of his age he had been given rare privileges about the establishment. And it had been due, not to his own remarkable ability, but to the fact that Tang from the first had been kindly disposed toward him. In the Classics the sages taught that ingratitude was one of the worst of all evils. His memory flashed to Den. How differently that one had tried to repay the man who had shown him such questionable friendliness. And Tang! Tang had advanced him whenever possible; Tang had given him the maximum in wages; Tang had even said that he trusted him as a son. Young Fu could not stand his own thoughts another minute. He caught up the two objects he had finished and went toward the coppersmith.

The other looked up at his approach, but said nothing. That the master had no intention of easing the way for this youth who stood in embarrassment before him was evident. Young Fu held out the two brasses. "I have worked hard to make these as they should be. Will you look at them and tell me what they still lack?"

"The first has the marks of anger on its surface. The second improves. Is that all?"

Young Fu swallowed his pride. "I have been a fool!"

"Truly!" Then at the expression on the other's countenance, Tang relented. "And you do not think today that you know more about this business than do I?"

"Only today have I realized how stupid I have been."

"You think that you might still learn a few things?"

The youth nodded miserably.

"Then return to the anvil for a few days and prove the truth of this."

Young Fu obeyed. He was far from happy, but his wretchedness had lessened. He set about the work in a new spirit.

Three days later, Lu was welcomed back to the shop. The tall form had lost its burden of worry. Except for a few added lines about his eyes, Lu appeared much the same as when he was hurried off to the ya-men. He lifted a piece of Young Fu's work in amazement, "You did not do this, certainly?"

Old Tsu interrupted humorously, "Difficult as it is to believe, the countryman is now wedded to his anvil. My position as designer is once more safe, but unless you speedily prove your ability, yours will be gone."

Tang added his contribution, "A little surprise I kept for your return, Lu, a poor workman turned into a good one." His eyes never left the youth's face. What he saw there seemed to satisfy him, for later he said, "When you have finished what you are doing, Young Fu, I have other work for you."

When the article in hand was finished and Lu had again paid it a compliment, Young Fu went to Tang.

"I have an order for a tray," the coppersmith began, "something for which the purchaser is willing to pay well. If you have any ideas that are original, work them out and let me see." Tang was still businesslike, but Young Fu recognized this as a return to old responsibility. It was strange, though, that he had come to think of the anvil with a certain interest. It was, at least, not the one spot in the place to be avoided.

When he submitted the design, Tang examined it carefully. "This will do. See that your work on it is of the same quality."

Young Fu lost himself happily in the task. At night he figured what strokes would count for the most in the next day's cutting. He was so engrossed by the subject that one evening Fu Be Be spoke to him sharply, "Where are your wits? Three times have I told you that a message came today from my nephew in the hills. My sister-in-law has again been ill; this time she did not recover. Last night she left for the spirit world. Tomorrow at dawn I cross the river. So long as I can help them, I shall remain."

The next day he mentioned the matter of his mother's having gone. "Why not close the house and stay with me here?" asked the coppersmith when they were alone for a moment.

"You mean you wish me to sleep and eat with you while my mother is away?"

"Will that be such a hardship, that you hesitate about it?" Tang's eyes once more held their friendly warmth.

Fu Be Be stayed in the hills for ten days. Each night, with evening rice eaten, the three apprentices were left to their own amusement. Tang and Young Fu sat late talking of politics, of business, of the past years in Chungking as the older man had known them. Pulling at his water pipe, Tang grew reminiscent. "In the past ten years, even five, more has happened than in centuries preceding. The Middle Kingdom is in a new cycle of history; where it will lead is not for me to say. That out of this trouble will come a stable government, there is no doubt. Always before, order has resulted after long periods of banditry and warfare. It will be the same at this time. I, who have fifty years to my credit, may not live so long. But you are young."

"Eighteen and one-half years," Young Fu said, half to himself.

"Almost a man."

At the youth's rueful reception of this statement, the coppersmith laughed. "Few in Years, did you think I would grant you full maturity?"

"I am most unworthy of such honor, Respected Coppersmith, but," his eyes sparkled mischievously, "in the evenings past you have treated me like a man."

"Verily, in the hope that you might grow to fill the title!" Tang changed to seriousness. "What is your chief wish for the future?"

"Long ago I thought that some day I might like to open a shop of my own. At present I am not sure. Much money would be needed. Moreover," Young Fu colored slightly, "I am not unhappy here."

"Even when you have to take your turn at the anvil?"

"Even then. The anvil, I have found, is not so bad."

"No task into which a man puts his heart is too bad.

For the lazy, all work is difficult. 'The superior man finds pleasure in doing what is uncongenial'—a lesson you had to learn. So you are not unhappy in this place?" pursued Tang.

"No. There are many reasons. No shop in the province has so fine a reputation; the men are good to work with," he paused as if hunting for words to conclude this summary, "and you—" his voice faded away.

"You think I have not been too harsh a master?" the older man mused. "Long ago I told you that I trusted you as a son. I did not make that statement without some thought. When you needed punishment, I gave it as a father might have done. It was not entirely without pain to myself. Carefully have I watched you develop," his eyes smiled, "sometimes with deep anxiety! An overweening pride and a hot temper you have. The second I share with you; the first, life, given time, will rid you of thoroughly. I have, as you know, no one with blood claims. You have only your mother. If within this next year you continue to prove this manhood you are so anxious to assume, I shall recognize you as my son by the law of adoption. You will not win this without bitterness. I shall begin soon to place on your body some of the responsibility that now burdens my own shoulders, and there will come times when the anvil will seem a pleasant way of spending effort." He rose, put down his pipe, and stretched his arms. "Ai! but the hours fly! Tomorrow we shall neither of us do good work."

Young Fu stood silent before the other. "I have no words—"

He had wondered at the marvels of this city.

"None are needed," was the reply. "I am not so stupid as some may think." He glanced up whimsically, "Now go to sleep!"

Sleep was the last thing he wished to do, the youth felt at the moment. His pulse was beating so loudly that the apprentices, sound in slumber, might have heard it. As Tang's adopted son, his fortune was made. But that was not the important side of the affair. There was not the slightest doubt in his own mind of the coppersmith's feeling for him. This, a wisdom older than his years helped him to realize, would do more toward making him mature than any other force in his life. Tang would see, and soon, that he was a man deserving of a man's friendship. Tang! Tang's adopted son! He turned the words over and over on his tongue. Why should he alone of all Chungking's youth know such happiness?

And only five years ago he had stood that first night in Chair-Makers' Way and wondered at the marvels of this city. Nothing but good had come to him here. On occasion he had played with folly and twice, at least, the city had with a swift change of countenance threatened to ruin him. But such times had been few.

Noiselessly he rose and slipped to the window. Through the barred grating he could see the warm summer moon. Under its rays the roof tops sheltering a million Chungkingese had become darkly beautiful. For the present dinginess and squalor had disappeared, and the Lin and Yangtze had changed their muddy torrents, as if by magic, into streams of molten silver. Two or three hours for this unearthly glamour to linger, and then another dawn would sound its clarion for all who labored.

Young Fu's heart leaped at the thought. Tomorrow Fu Be Be would return to share his good fortune. Tomorrow he would begin to prove himself to Tang. Tomorrow—! Ai, but life was good!

GLOSSARY OF CHINESE WORDS
(*as used in Young Fu's time*)

AI-YA (ī=yä), an exclamation expressing surprise, dismay, and sometimes, anger.

A-MAH (ä′=ma), an Oriental term for nurse.

BAN-KEH (bän=kā), managing guest: a West China term for bandits.

CHUNGKING (chung-king), a city on the Yangtze in southwest China.

CHIN-T'SAI (chin=t'sī), a cheap, green vegetable grown in China.

DSEN-GIA-NGAI (dzen=jä=ngī), the name of a small village a short distance overland from Chungking.

DAI (dī), a proper name.

FU (foo), a proper name.

FU BE BE (foo bä bä), the last two syllables were attached to proper names to designate women of the working class.

FU YUIN-FAH (foo yoon=fä), surname and given name. In Chinese a surname always precedes a given name.

GONG HSI GO NIEN (gông shē gō nien), Greetings! Good Fortune for the New Year!

HOCHOW (hŏ′jō), a small city on the Lin River.

HSIEN-SENG (shen=sung), a title meaning teacher or gentleman.

KWEI (gwä), an evil spirit; a devil.

Kweichow (gwā-jō), a province southeast of Szechuen.

Kuailai (kwī=lī), Come quickly!

Lao-Po-Po (lou=pō'=pō), a title meaning old grandmother.

Li (lē), a proper name. Also the word for one-third mile.

Ling (ling), a proper name.

Liu (lē'yoo), a proper name.

Lu (loo), a proper name.

Mei-shiang-tz (mā=shiang=tz), a large basket with a hinged lid, sometimes round and sometimes square.

Ma teh fah (mē dā fä), a contraction for "muh iu fah tz," meaning "there is no help for it": used in and around Chungking.

Pu-gai (poo'=gī), a comfort stuffed with cotton, wool, or silk waste.

San-Tz-Ching (san=tz=jing), the Three Characters Primer.

Shi chi deh hun (shē' chē dā hun'), very strange; queer.

Si-Mu (su'=moo), a title meaning married woman of the upper class.

Szechuen (se'chuän), an extremely large province of West China.

Tang (täng), a proper name.

Tang Yu-shu (täng yü=shü), surname and given name.

T'sai-feng (t'sĭ'=fung), a tailor.

Tsu (dzoo), a proper name.

Tuchun (doo'jun), a military governor of a province.

Tu-To (too=tō), a small city on the Lin River, northwest of Chungking.

Wang (wäng), a proper name.

GLOSSARY OF CHINESE WORDS

Wu (woo), a proper name.

Ya-men (yä'=mun), an official residence containing police court, prisons, etc.

Yunnan (yün-nan'), a province southwest of Szechuen.

Yangtze (yang'tz), the name of China's greatest river. It rises in the mountains of Tibet and flows for more than two thousand miles before it empties into the Pacific Ocean.

Where no accent marks are placed, it means an equal accent on every syllable.

NOTES

The following comments by Alison R. Lanier incorporate information from the Notes in the 1932 edition of this book and contrast life in China then and now. Conditions there may change and the China of tomorrow will probably be different than it is today.

China has changed a lot since this book was written. Where once there were fierce warlords fighting for power in all parts of the land, now there is a strong and highly controlled central government. Where once there were clear-cut levels, from very rich to wretchedly poor, China has now been "leveled" to one plateau, where no one is either rich or poor and everyone is equally a worker, working for the State and not himself. Where once many Chinese died from hunger and people lived in fear of both flood and famine, now food is plentiful, rivers are controlled, and fields are irrigated.

During World War II, when the Japanese held much of China, Chinese Communists established themselves far off in the remote North. The Chinese Nationalists, under the leadership of Chiang Kai-shek, established themselves far in the west of China. When Japan was defeated (in 1945), the Communists, led by Mao Tse-tung, came out of their stronghold and continued their struggle for domination of mainland China against Chiang Kai-shek. They gradually brought the whole country under their control after long hard fighting, and on October 1, 1949, proclaimed a new China. Chiang Kai-shek and his forces withdrew to the island of Taiwan. "The People's

Republic of China" is now a totally Communist country. That means the entire economy—all factories, railroads, large farms, large stores, everything—is owned and run by the government, not by private people.

Young Fu would find it a different world. He would not fight bandits in the streets nor would he flee in the night from the river's terror. Also, however, he would not be able to choose where he and his mother would live, he could not select his trade or express his own desire to design and create, nor could he work up his pay and responsibility until he finally inherited the shop.

The following notes describe some of the many changes that have come over this vast country. It is important to understand that this book is a picture of the past, a picture full of lights and shadows, of beauty and despair. Today's China is healthier, for most people it is more secure. The lights have been dimmed but so have the shadows.

Some things have been lost from Young Fu's China, some things have been gained. Readers might enjoy considering the many ways in which his life would have been different had he lived today instead of in the early part of this century.

CHAPTER I

TRANSPORTATION

Most of China's transportation used to be by water, and much still is. Roads out in the countryside are usually of dirt or stone, and very narrow, but in the towns and cities they are being rebuilt afresh. Men carry great weights swung from poles that rest on their shoulders, as is done all over Asia. They push wheelbarrows which passengers and supplies share equally.

They harness themselves with ropes to drag huge logs or blocks of stone.

Men used to carry sedan chairs in which people rode, and pull jinrikishas, or tiny carriages, but they no longer do this.

Nowadays roads are being built for cars, especially through the east where the largest cities are located. There still are not many private cars, but there are increasing numbers of trucks, and in the cities people move about in gas-motored buses or electric trolley buses powered by overhead lines. These buses are solid, clean, and Chinese-built, with big wide windows. Most people still move about on foot, however, in such great numbers that they almost choke the roadways. Thousands more travel by bicycle, oxcart, donkey cart or behind horses. In Peking there is a subway with palatial stations, decorated with murals, softly lit, and offering music. There are, however, only fifteen miles of track. People ride it for fun; it costs only two cents.

Those who want to travel long distances can do so now by train. The railway network covers all of China except Tibet, though it is densest in the northeast. From Peking to Shanghai (926 miles) takes 23 hours; from Peking to Moscow about seven days. So those who can afford it fly. Planes reach almost any part of China the same day. Many of the planes are British turbo-jets; others are of Russian make.

CHAPTER II

EDUCATION

Learning was limited, until the revolution, to families of wealth and social position. This was due to the fact that the Chinese written language, ideographs, requires long and intensive study for its mastery. For this the majority of the population could not pay. Accordingly, through the centuries, scholarship and scholars were esteemed above all else in life.

But in the New China this has changed, and scholarship is no longer revered for its own sake. Art, calligraphy, classics, and history are not taught as they once were. Now everything is learned for the use of the State, so it must all be related to some form of work. Today all children in China attend school from babyhood up, but much of their school time is spent in work in factories or fields or army drill rather than in study. When young people finish high school they cannot go right to college. Instead they must work at least two years. After this they may perhaps go to college, but only if their fellow workers select them. This happens only if they have been completely loyal to the State, and if their thinking is considered politically correct.

From the earliest days of nursery school, children are taught the thinking of the leader, Mao Tse-tung. They memorize his teachings; even toddlers learn songs that teach his political views. All education is planned to make the children proud to live and work for China, not for themselves or their families. By such teaching at every level, in every corner of China, the new regime has harnessed a tremendous, unified, and obedient force to build a new nation.

COINAGE

It used to be that each province in China had its own money. Sometimes the coins were made of silver, sometimes of copper. They were of various designs depending on the province. Now all China uses the same coinage, which is called "Renminbi," shortened in writing to RMB, and also referred to as Yuan. This money cannot be taken out of China. There are roughly 2 RMB to a U.S. dollar (1972).

STREETS

In Young Fu's day, streets in China were narrow and winding; pedestrians squeezed their bodies against walls or shop fronts to avoid dangerous collisions. Streets changed their direction frequently at sharp angles, as a protection against evil spirits who, it was believed, could travel only in a straight line and would therefore dash themselves to ruin against the first solid barrier.

Reminders of the old personality of each city still linger in the back streets, side alleys, and some of the old shopping streets, but much has been torn down to make room for factories and massive rectangular modern apartment houses. Main roads and broad new thoroughfares cut through most cities now, replacing the walls that once divided cities, or surrounded and protected them. The Chinese are planting innumerable trees everywhere which will grow and someday shade the roads.

SUPERSTITIONS AND "THE FOUR OLDS"

In Young Fu's time, Chinese life was permeated by the fear of evil spirits. It was widely believed, especially among the lower classes, that the Dragon, an enormous power for evil, controlled the elements and dwelt in the waterways and mountains. The Dragon terrorized those who feared him into inactivity at time of danger.

Superstitions have since been cast out of Chinese thinking—there are no more dragons or imaginary evil spirits.

When the leaders decided to create a New China, they felt they had to totally wipe out what they called "The Four Olds": old ideas, old culture, old customs, old habits.

To do this, in 1966 they launched what was called "The Cultural Revolution." It still continues in a quieter form, but

261

for two years, from 1966 to 1968, there were terror and chaos. The young people, called "Red Guards," were encouraged to rampage across the country, eradicating everything that remained of old religious practices, old superstitions, old festivals, old ways of dress, old traditions. They burst into homes and public buildings, smashing, destroying, terrorizing. They burned books in huge bonfires, hacked down old statues, slashed old paintings, cut old scrolls to ribbons. They invaded people's homes without warning to tear out family shrines in order to break up ancestor worship. Churches and temples were turned into warehouses, basketball courts, or barns for animals.

Once Chinese women wore lovely brocaded dresses, jewelry, and cosmetics. Now they wear the same shapeless blue or gray trousers and shirts as the men; one rarely sees rouge, lipstick, or curled hair.

Old Chinese literature is not available; what you find in every bookstore are the works of Chairman Mao and sometimes a few periodicals on politics, medicine, agriculture, or similar useful matters. All the classic old plays, opera, and traditional music are gone. Only ten standard musical works are allowed, all propaganda pieces for the New China. These are played over and over again, either in full or in sections. There are no longer family ceremonies connected with weddings or funerals; everything traditional has been carefully stamped out.

CHAPTER III

FOOT BINDING

This is now past history; in fact, the Chinese are a little ashamed that they ever did such a painful and harmful thing to women.

NOTES

CHAPTER IV

Beggars and Bandits

At the time this book was written, beggars and bandits were a frightening part of everyone's life. They were everywhere. It was estimated that approximately one-third of the population was actively engaged in banditry. For a number of years China was plunged in civil warfare. People were looted so often that in desperation the law-abiding often turned to robbery as a means of livelihood. Soldiers, cheated of pay for months at a time, joined these bands.

Nowadays everybody in China works. Every person is accounted for and is part either of a "commune" (or community) in the country or a "street" (or district) in the cities. Central Committee representatives keep track of each person; they make sure that everybody is working to help rebuild China. The devastating poverty of the past no longer exists.

CHAPTER V

Sanitation

In Young Fu's day there was no such thing as sanitation in China, except in a few of the great cities like Shanghai, Nanking, and Peiping (now called Peking). There was no plumbing or sewage in the countryside; every kind of waste was carried from houses in buckets by coolies and sold to feed hogs or as fertilizer for farmers. Water was carried from streams, lakes, and rivers and sold at so much per bucket. Cities had no responsibility in such matters; each individual householder provided his own service.

The most visible change in New China is cleanliness. Everything sparkles and shines, even train floors, the railway stations, the front steps of people's houses. Everyone is responsible for seeing that his house or farm or office or shop is spotless.

In many places outside the large cities, water must still be carried. Squatting women beat their clothes clean on rocks by a stream. Human fertilizer is collected and carried to the fields in wooden buckets. But people are clean, farms are clean, and even the streets are constantly swept and kept free of papers and dirt.

CHAPTER IX

FLOODS

China's great rivers, especially the Yangtze and the Yellow, used to devastate the land and claim numerous victims at periodic intervals. In modern times, along every major river, thousands upon thousands of people carrying rocks and gravel in baskets on their heads worked until they actually collapsed. Through this gigantic effort, the New Chinese have dammed rivers, built reservoirs, and dug countless miles of irrigation ditches all over China. No longer are floods a constant terror in the land.

Now, when any river rises, the water is trapped behind these new dams. Then it is released carefully, according to a plan, into the reservoirs. There it stays until it is needed. Later in the year, when rivers run dry and when formerly there would have been disastrous droughts and famines, the stored water is released into the long miles of ditches so it can irrigate the farms. Modern Chinese no longer dread the famines that used to follow long dry spells, bringing hunger, misery, and death to wide areas of China.

NOTES

REVERENCE FOR AGE

Chinese respect for age reverts to Confucius' teachings concerning the treatment of elders and the worship of ancestors. In the Chinese mind, age and wisdom were always linked together.

Nowadays people's worth depends on their capacity to produce and help build China. So old people no longer have the revered place they once did. They keep on working as long as they are able to do so. When they are too old to work, grandparents often settle in with their children so that they can look after the grandchildren. In this way they can still be useful, making it easier for the parents to do still more outside the home. Most families have only one room that must serve as both a living room and a bedroom. But when grandparents move in, the family can usually get permission to have an extra room.

Chinese enjoy family life; ties are still very strong, and children remain loyal and close to their parents even though they no longer worship ancestors as they once did. The mounds of ancient family graves have now been cleared away so more land can be tilled; family shrines in homes have been replaced by portraits of Chairman Mao. But young people still respect their elders; they look after them when they are sick or in trouble. The only ones who go to Old People's Homes are those who have no children to look after them, or who are so sick they cannot be cared for at home.

CHAPTER XIII

MARRIAGE CUSTOMS

Traditionally, all Chinese marriages were arranged by the parents or guardians of the young people involved. Frequently friends, having a son in one household and a daughter in the other, would "betroth" their two children when only a few years old. A girl on her marriage day gave up her own home and family and went to her new home, which was that of her husband's family, to become a member of that one, just as though her own family had ceased to exist.

In the 1930's this began to change as young people selected their own spouses and some built homes of their own rather than live with the husband's family.

The modern Chinese State realizes that people work better if they are happily settled, so it encourages marriage, but only when a couple is in their late twenties. You do not see boys and girls holding hands or courting very much. Sometimes they walk together, looking very "uni-sex" in their look-alike clothes, or they go together to a theater or wait to sit next to each other at a political performance in the factory auditorium. Now and then young people can walk together on the mass organized hikes that are taken for physical fitness, or on the way to do a day's work on some far-away farm.

But romance is not allowed to be part of today's life. When a couple gets married there is no party, no gay celebration. The couple goes to a government office or the farm center where they work and signs a book together. That is all. They do not often get divorced, but if this occurs, they just go back to the same office and cancel out their registration—though a social worker tries to persuade them not to do that.

If the government needs one of them in another part of China, that person goes to his or her new assignment, even if it means breaking up the family. In that case, the family is given a month together once a year and train fare home is provided.

MISCELLANEOUS

ASCEND THE DRAGON. An expression meaning to die.
GUILD. An organization similar to a labor union.

At the time this book was written, no rest day was observed, except where there was strong foreign influence. Men worked every day in the year save Feast Days. Today everyone works at least six days a week and often attends political meetings on the seventh.

ABOUT THE AUTHOR

As a young woman, Elizabeth Foreman Lewis worked in various fields: architectural designs for doll houses, railroad statistics, and institutional work in a Slavic settlement. She received special training in religious education, Bible and English literature, and in 1917 was sent to China by the Methodist Women's Board. There she studied the Chinese language and history and held several posts in Shanghai, Chunking and Nanking. In Nanking she taught in the Girls' Boarding School and later in the Boys' Academy. In 1921 she married John Abraham Lewis, principal of the Academy.

Upon her return to the United States because of illness, Mrs. Lewis wrote short stories for six years and then wrote her first book, YOUNG FU OF THE UPPER YANGTZE, which was awarded the John Newbery Medal in 1932. This book, along with others by Mrs. Lewis, was published widely abroad and transcribed into Braille. Most of her short stories have been included in anthologies.

Later came other books for children, including HO-MING, GIRL OF CHINA and TO BEAT A TIGER, books for adults and more short stories. Mrs. Lewis died in 1958 at the age of sixty-six in Baltimore, the city of her birth.

ABOUT THE ARTIST

Ed Young was born and grew up in Shanghai, China. At the age of twenty he came to the United States and studied at the University of Illinois and at the Art Center College in Los Angeles. Mr. Young is the illustrator of THE EMPEROR AND THE KITE, a Caldecott Honor Book, and many other notable books for children.